Puthur Zoological Park

(Hand in Hand, Paw in Paw)

Written by **C. R. Das**
Translated & Illustrated by **Austin Ajit**

Ukiyoto Publishing

*Dedicated to all the suffering and innocent animals
in the world.*

Foreword

<u>**The Mute and Dreary**</u>

Human beings enjoy all the privileges for being the supreme masters of the universe, as they have the largest brain. Humans make use of everything under the sun. Men learned to ease their work by using animals by domestication when they started farming.

But later, most of the domesticated animals were forced to become draft animals. As they are mute and are unableto show feelings humans are treating them as slaves. This book is a heartrending novel of a wild chimp who was caught in a net and had to lead a very unfortunate life in a local roadside circus. Roadside 'circus show' was very common in the past in which mostly chained monkeys were trained to do some tricks. The show will be performed where people gather.

This translation "Puthur Zoological park"is done by the child author Master Austin Ajit who is a nature enthusiast . He believes that humans always abuse and disturb the law of nature by invading animal territories, and they were the root cause of many species's extinction.

If only animal could talk, they would have protested the brutal behavior of humans.

The new generation children may not be so familiar with the once popular circus shows. Back then children were the main spectators then. The show consists of many tricks and amazing acrobats by men, women and children and the core attraction was the many tricks by animals. Animals and birds were performing humanly tricks only by fear. They are held in captivity and are trained by humans who torture them. The helpless animals obey only because of the pain and fear.

In this book, the master Palani taught some tricks to the monkeys to perform which earned him money. He looks after them well but, a drunk Palani beats them up black and blue. The chimp recollects its native forest life where it lived in the protection of its mother. The author introduces many animals and birds and gives an idea of separate territories.

The dramatic explanations give the reader a world of its own where animals are also have feelings like humans. Though they live under nature's law fulfilling their basic needs and instincts, we human beings can relate every incident with reality.

Austin Ajit is a marvelous author who accomplished many books on different subjects. This translation from Malayalam "Puthur Zoological park throws light to a past when these circus shows were very common but brutal.

The Malayalam Author Sri.C R Das is an environment enthusiast and animal lover. This book may be a tribute to those animals and birds who were trapped and confined in human hands from their natural habitat.

This is a must-read book which is crafted intellectually by the brilliant little master Austin Ajit. I am so happy to write a small note for this and I wish him all the very best for his future literary works.

Briji K T

Bengaluru.

BRIJI.K.T is a bilingual writer and an artist. Her books are published by leading publishers like Ukiyoto Publishers, Poornna publishers, Saikatham Publishers, Buddha books, Red Cherry books and by the "Institute for children's literature" Kerala Gov. In the platform of art, she has conducted several exhibitions.

Translator's note

While Mittu, Chimpu, and everyone else in this story are fictional, the situations aren't.Animals really do get tortured by us humans. They get kidnapped from home, either to be sold as pets to some rich person (who often mistreat and ignore their pet), or to function as a slave. Circus animals (while now banned) were tortured even worse. All the cruel techniques of the circus trainers mention are real! And, the worst part is, they were rewarded by their crimes! Zoos are no better. While some zoos are better than others, some are horrible!

I mean, imagine this: You are kidnapped from your home, forced to stay in a cooped-up cage, with horrible food. Animals threw stones at you, and you are confined to that place for the rest of your life. Sound nice? Well, that's what happens to some zoo animals. Not to mention the fact that at the same time we are destroying their habitat, replacing them with cities and farms, and murdering them simply because we want their bones, skin, etc.

Truly, we humans have been horrible to animals. And they can't cry out for their justice. That's what makes this book important, and it's why I translated it.

The message of unity and the suffering of animals are both things humans can learn from. Humans have no unity and kill their own people in wars. And we treat all life forms other than us as 'lesser' or 'foolish'. So don't be like a normal human, and smile as they cry. Try and spread the reality and try and make these poor creature's lives bearable. For they too are alive and can feel pain.

So next time you see an animal in a zoo, or go to ride an elephant or horse, think for a second about their life, and how they suffer for your enjoyment.

Austin Ajit.

Contents

Part One: Chimpu

Chapter 1: The Circus

"Thoom, THOOM- THOOM!". The sound of Palani's drums reverberated in the air. Kutti Raman, the little monkey, hopped around, dancing and playing his tambourine. *Chin-chink! THUD! Chin-chink!* it went. Chimpu the chimpanzee sat and watched as the duo's music rose into the air, making an exciting atmosphere. The tension was electric.

Kids poured out of schools and colleges, at the ring of the bell. It was five o'clock. Street kids were the first to arrive. They watched as Kutti Raman jumped about, playing his instrument.

Today was the day! The one and only day! The day that rules days!

'What day is it?', you might ask. Well, a Sunday! Oh, wait, that's not what you meant. Well, on that day was… The first ever show of the one and only… CHIMPU-CIRCUS! YAY! Set in the Thekkinkadu Maidan, it was small but strong.

More kids poured into the circus, as the drums hypnotized passers-by.

"THOOOM-THOOM-THOOM-THUD-THUD-THOOM!". The drumming increased at a furious pace. Chimpu sat, smirking. It was as if he was the master of this circus! Suddenly, the drumming stopped. Palani reached into his pocket, and pulled out a cigar. He lit it and smoked it for a while, before handing it to Chimpu. He smoked with great gusto. Kutti Raman looked wistfully at the cigar, and held his hand out for it. Chimpu looked angry, and slapped Kutti Raman away. "THIS IS MINE!" He seemed to say. The poor little monkey's wail echoed around, as more people gathered to watch this strange show!

 Palani announced in a grand mix of Tamil and Malayalam "Welcome all to the one and only Chimpu Circus! Meet my good friend, Chimpu the chimpanzee. He's a strong fella, but is quite like you and me! Here's his companion, Kutti Raman the monkey! To earn a living and fill our three tummies, we shall preform all sorts of tricks for you, dear audience! Nowhere else will you meet a chimpanzee like our Chimpu! So stand back, please, and let the show begin!".

The drums began again, but instead of taking a step back, everyone jostled to get closer. Chimpu and Kutti Raman stood up, and the audience fell back. They were a tiny bit scared of the two animals.

Palani started ordering everyone where to sit. "Let the children sit in the front, for they should be able to see and enjoy the show! Please sit down everyone— No, not there, a bit to the left. What did I just say? Sit DOWN please, or we won't begin! Sir, please remove your hat, for it is blocking the view of others. And you madam, must move a bit to the right. Yes, that's better".

Then, once everyone settled down, the first act began— Kutti Raman's act! Chimpu was handed the drums, which he beated rhythmically. The crowd was astonished at this. A chimp, playing a drum so well? More and more people flocked to the circus to see this sight.

Kutti Raman took up a kavadi offering and began dancing the traditional dance of *Kavadi Aattam*. Palani picked up a trumpet and began blowing different tunes. As each tune changed, so did Kutti Raman! He turned into a doctor, then a driver, a sage, a mage, a beggar, a person named McGregor, as Hanuman, even as Palani himself!

He even managed to disappear, only to re-appear in the audience, disguised as a human! He was so good at acting that no one noticed him sneak into the seats.

He did many such imitations, all of which were so realistic and shocking that the crowd gasped at each one! Finally, Kutti Raman fell to the ground, motionless. He was dead… or was he? The crowd wept for the monkey. Then Chimpu leaped down and placed Kutti Raman into a coffin. Then, Palani asked the crowd for coins, to help him and his monkeys survive. The crowd tossed coins, and Chimpu picked them up. Then, out of the blue, Kutti Raman burst out of the coffin like a super hero, and took a few coins for himself! He dragged most of the coins away, and when Chimpu came to take them, he leaped into the coffin and closed the lid! The crowd roared with laughter, showering even more coins!

"Thank you, thank you! Now, a little act of mine…" said Palani. He took out two glass bottles from a box, each one filled with water and fish. Palani told Chimpu to play faster, and the drumming intensified.

"I shall drink these fish—alive!". The audience were at the edge of their seat in anticipation. Suddenly, Palani held out his hand, and Chimpu's drumming stopped. Palani calmly poured a cup of live fish (and a bit of water), and gulped it down.

The audience gasped!

Then, noticing a suspicious figure in the crowd, Palani said "By the way, this area is filled with pickpockets, so take care of your purses". Then, as the crowd quickly made sure their purses and bags were safe, Palani gulped down one, two, three, four, five, six more fishes! Soon, the bottles were empty. Suddenly, as he gulped the last fish, Palani froze, and fell with a thud! The crowd screamed! Was he okay? Chimpu stopped drumming, and picked up a medical kit. He took a stethoscope, and checked Palani's heartbeat. Then, Chimpu took out a syringe, and injected Palani. He got up with a start! Then, he spat out all the fishes into a tray. The crowd sighed in relief, and clapped wildly.

Then, it was Chimpu's turn. First, he took a cigarette and smoked it like a gangster. Then, he took multiple cigarettes, smoking each one in a different way. He smoked multiple at once, then used them as fangs, and did all sorts of antics.

"Monkey man!" exclaimed the crowd, as more and more people came to see this so called human-monkey.

Chimpu then balanced three hats on his head, hands and feet! He did a handstand, then a leg stand (aka just standing normally) then a head stand!

YEAH!
WOW!
CHIMPU'S
CIRCUS
THE BEST!
LOOL!

Finally, Palani announced the last trick. "This is the last trick of the day, so let's all give our Chimpu and Kutti Raman here some encouragement!". He took out a long stick with a metal end on one side. Chimpu changed into a shirt and pant, along with a small hat. He looked like a little human! As the audience whispered with anticipation, Palani balanced that metal stick upright on Chimpu's shoulder, and let it go. It stood straight, like a tree growing straight out of his shoulder. Then, Kutti Raman climbed to the top of the stick (still upright) and balanced on it! The crowd held their breath. Then, Kutti Raman tied his belt to the end of the still straight stick, and span on it like a windmill! He rotated and posed like a flying superman (or super monkey, to be precise)! Palani changed the tempo of the drum, and Kutti Raman spun faster and slower. Suddenly, Chimpu knocked the stick off his shoulder with a quick swipe, and Kutti Raman fell… right into Chimpu's arms. The two bowed, and the audience exploded into applause, showering them with coins! Confetti exploded all over the ground, and with another bow, Chimpu and Kutti Raman cartwheeled into a tent.

Palani patted the two, before announcing that today's show was over. But the crowd did not want to leave! They loved Palani, Chimpu and Kutti Raman's circus too much!

Palani had tied a little cloth tent underneath a mango tree. Once everyone finally left, Palani put all the equipment back into their boxes, and tied Chimpu and Kutti Raman inside the tent (this was not unkind, but instead to keep them safe from people, cars, etc). Palani hugged the two, saying "It's all because of you two and your talent that we keep on surviving!"

Then, he brought bread, biscuits, tasty treats, and bananas for them to feast on. Palani then counted his coins, and went to the city.

Chapter 2: The City

"La-LA LAAAAA! Loo-Leee LAAA! Lalalalaaaaaaa!". Kutti Raman and Chimpu, who were nearly asleep, shot up, onto their feet. It was night time, and Palani was back. Only it wasn't Palani.

After his trips to the city, the kind Palani would disappear, replaced by a monster. He would scream and kick and swear until dawn broke, after which his drunken stupor would shatter. He reverted to his normal self. Chimpu and Kutti Raman feared this drunk Palani. He was a demon! A devil! A monkey-kicker! A... a drunk Demon! Oh, if only he wouldn't drink so much. Maybe then he would be kinder. But 'if only's and 'maybe's don't help anyone. So, for now, Palani was a monster.

Still singing, he bent down and entered the tent. Then, seeing Kutti Raman and Chimpu chilling there, he got infuriated. Why? The two poor monkeys had no idea. Swearing, Palani picked up poor Kutti Raman and threw him out of the tent, with a throw that any javelin player would be proud off. Then, his rage turned to Chimpu.

"EEK! EEEEK! AEEEEK!" Screeched the poor ape as he was kicked repeatedly by the drunk demon who currently controlled Palani. He soon joined Kutti Raman outside, and the poor duo sat in misery. Then, still needing to ruin someone's day, Palani came out and began yelling at people passing by.

Poor Kutti Raman and Chimpu fell asleep, with the clangs of the municipal clock reaching 4 AM ringing in their ears. When they woke up, the sun was blasting at their face. Morning had arrived. Kutti Raman huddled in a corner, shaking with fear.

Palani lay, in a deep sleep. His front teeth poked out, and his smallpox scars were as ugly as ever. Whenever Palani drank alcohol, he went crazy.

■■■

It was 8:00AM. Palani awoke from his slumber when Chimpu began screeching. He was hungry! Palani woke up, and stared at the two with remorse. He petted them, saying "Yesterday, I hurt you both too much. I am sorry, I…I…" he began crying. Kutti Raman comforted him, and Palani hugged the two. He got up and bought some idlis, and a few bananas. He ate with Chimpu and Kutti Raman. Then, he got them all tea!

Later, he said I'll have to go for a long time, so don't worry! Stay here". He tied the two with a long chain (so they could walk out of the tent) and went. The two sat there for a while, picking lice out of their fur, and wondering about things. Then, they went outside, where they heard… Crying?

Under a tree nearby was a small baby, sleeping soundly in a cradle. But it was not he who was crying. Beside him sat his older sister and a three year old boy. It was he who was wailing. Chimpu beckoned them towards him, hooting like a flute.

The boy and girl came nearby. Seeing Kutti Raman and Chimpu, the boy stopped crying, and stared at them quizzically. Seeing how thin and scrawny they were, Chimpu realized they were hungry.

Chimpu scampered back inside the tent, coming back with a banana in his hands. His shoved it at the girl, who hesitantly took it from him. The boy wolfed down the banana. The boy began crying for another, which was given this time by Kutti Raman. Soon this too was devoured. Now the boy was satisfied. The girl referred to the boy as 'Muni', and herself as 'Ponni'.

To entertain them, Kutti Raman jumped and summersaulted! Muni raised his eyebrows, before copying the same summersault. Ponni began singing a Tamil song, and Chimpu began drumming to its rhythm… upside down! Onlookers watched in awe. It was truly a sight to see! They sang and played for the rest of the day.

■■

Muni and Ponni didn't know where exactly they were from. Their parents sold pearl necklaces and beads, and went to sell things early morning. They left the baby in a cradle , wrapped in a sari. The children lived in the Maidan by themselves most of the time, and to them, the world was just the ground and the sky. They had never seen anything but that.

Muni was a smart fellow. But his shirt was barely a scrap of fabric, and he barely had any belongings. He had a slingshot that he took from his sister, which he used to annoy the baby. When he did, the baby would cry and Ponni would scold Muni. The whole thing escalated until everyone was crying. Life was such, for them. It was hard.

Chimpu liked Ponni. Even if he couldn't talk, the chimp could understand human words really well. And even then, he could communicate through sounds and sign language. Ponni was a kind child, but she was thin and starving, with dirty black hair and sad eyes.

■■

After the two children left, Chimpu watched as cars and busses whizzed by on the road. Chimpu found cities to be a strange land, with roads snaking around the place like rivers made of asphalt. Cars and buses drove around like shoals of fish. Despite the name, Thekkinkadu Maidan had no teak trees. Thekk means teak tree, and kadu means forest! But the area was dry and barren, like an island surrounded by an ocean of asphalt. However, there was a temple nearby which was surrounded by trees. Banyans, Royal Poinciana (*Chimpu tried pronouncing that. He couldn't figure it out. The best he found was 'Royal Poy-in-key-ana'. It seemed wrong, but how else could he pronounce it?*), mango, coconut, palm tree, you name it! The area was littered with small shops, and there were also nomadic people, with no real home or identity. Palani, Muni and Ponni, even Chimpu and Kutti Raman were all nomads, with no real permanent home.

Chapter 3: The Saviour

Chimpu and Kutti Raman were asleep, when a scream awoke them yet again. Chimpu shot up, awake, and jumped out. He saw a crowd gathering – and Ponni, screaming "LEAVE MY BROTHER ALONE!". A man with a pointy mustache was grabbing Muni and dragging him away. A kidnapper. The man kicked and put a hand over Muni's mouth, and carried him away. HOW DARE HE!

In an instant, Chimpu leapt out like a kung-fu master, shattering the chain binding him. He chased after the man.

People watched as Chimpu ran, and ran, and ran, never stopping. One guy munched on popcorn, saying 'this is the more exciting than a movie!'.

The kidnapper bolted, jumping into an auto-rickshaw. "START THE ENGINE" Yelled the man. But Chimpu was already on him. "BOOM!". The auto-driver was knocked out of the seat. Chimpu was the driver now! The man tossed poor Muni (who was bleeding from a cut) away, cursing. He took out a gun and aimed at Chimpu. But Chimpu was too smart. He ripped off the steering wheel and knocked the gun out of his hands. The man drew a knife, and raised his hand to stab Chimpu.

Chimpu froze, scared. Suddenly, as quick as a flash, the man ran out. Recovering from his fear, Chimpu roared louder than any lion, and leaped at the fleeing man. The clang of the metal steering wheel and the knife hitting each other resounded everywhere. The man tried to stab Chimpu, but he was blocked. Fencing like a professional, Chimpu pushed the man backwards. He tried to flee, but Chimpu knocked him out, smashing the steering wheel onto his skull. Wow, who knew a steering wheel was such an effective weapon? The man seemed unconscious, but Chimpu bit the man's ankle for good measure.

Soon, the crowd and police caught up and arrested the man. Then, holding Chimpu and Muni up into the air, they celebrated this super-hero chimp!

When Ponni got Muni back, she wept in joy. Apparently, this man was stalking the area for a while. He had offered Ponni some candy, but Ponni knew how twisted people could be, and declined. But she never expected the man to attack and drag away Muni. There were marks where the man had kicked her.

By then, it was time for the circus to begin! Palani came, confused by the crowd. *"What had Chimpu done? Did he attack someone?"* wondered Palani. He saw the broken chain and became furious. Not again! He stormed over to Chimpu, asking

"WHAT DID YOU DO, APE? WHAT HAVE YOU DONE?". You could practically see steam coming out of his ears. A nearby person came and told him everything. Hearing the truth, Palani hugged Chimpu and became very happy. "Oh, Chimpu!" exclaimed Palani.

The circus began. More people came than ever! Some people gave Chimpu and Kutti Raman bananas, and all was well until a police jeep arrived.

Palani froze, terrified. *"Had the municipality told the police about Chimpu, and his lack of a permit?"* he wondered, shivering at the thought. Instead of taking Chimpu away, the policemen congratulated them! The Circle Inspector even took a photo with Chimpu! Soon, news reporters and photographers came. It was the best moment of Chimpu and Palani's life. Now, there was no need to fear policemen anymore.

■■

That night, Palani came from his drinking expeditions late.

Before that, Ponni and Muni's parents came and thanked Chimpu and Kutti Raman. After that, it was like usual: Palani came in a half-alive way, beat both Kutti Raman and Chimpu to an ape and monkey pulp, and slept. But that morning, Vasu

,their friendly neighborhood tea-seller came with the newspaper. Much to Chimpu's shock, on the front page was the Circle Inspector and Chimpu's photo. On another newspaper, it said "Chimp saves orphan boy!".

Apparently, the person Chimpu caught was called Avinash. He was part of a local kidnapping gang.

Thanks to his capture, the police were able to find all of the gang, and make them pay for their crimes! That day was a busy one, with people coming from all over to see Chimpu. He didn't even get time to visit Ponni and Muni! The earnings of the circus increased, and so did the Chimpu-fans. But Palani's drinking also increased. Now, he barely talked, and it was then, he began coughing…

Chapter 4: The Hospital

When evening comes with its breeze, so do people. They flock to the grounds, some to enjoy the breeze, others to sit and bask in the sun. That day, Palani began preforming tricks to attract people. Chimpu and Kutti Raman became clowns, and Kutti Raman had a sign on his neck, saying "CHIMPU CIRCUS! The one and only!". This new form of advertising attracted lots of people.

Palani was not like his normal self. He looked sickly. He sat on a corner, playing a drum. Chimpu, on the other hand, was as lively as ever! He said Namaste to everyone, before taking an iron hoop and covering it with kerosene oil. Then, he lit it on fire, an held it up. Then Kutti Raman jumped through it! He jumped again, and again, then he danced through it, cannon-balled through it, and even jumped through it in a sitting position! Then, it was Chimpu's turn. He tied a rope-tail to himself, and took a club that looked like it was Hanumans! Then, Kutti Raman poured kerosene over the tail and lit fire on it. All the while, Palani sat, his face slack on the drum. He announced the last trick, and the drumming began.

Chimpu took a long pole, and Kutti Raman climbed it, when the drumming stopped. Palani collapsed, unconscious. Chimpu tossed away the pole, and he and Kutti Raman rushed over to their friend. Some of the audience helped him up, and took him to the hospital.

At first, Chimpu followed the audience, but a watch-guard shooed him away. Chimpu could not bear being away from his master, and so he climbed up the wall until he reached the top, and entered the hospital. He sat next to the unconscious Palani, nudging him. He whimpered. Suddenly, people began screaming. "MONKEY! AAAAH! IT'S AN EVIL WILD MONKEY! KILL IT!".

A man with a stick chased the poor chimpanzee out, and Chimpu ran, and ran, until he reached their tent. Inside, the kind audience had kept all the equipment back in their boxes.

Kutti Raman sat, crying, inside. Chimpu tried to comfort him, and the two hugged each other. Ponni and Muni, along with their parents tried to comfort them, giving them food. But the two didn't eat nor sleep, and just cried the night away.

That morning, Ponni came with idilis for the two. Chimpu and Kutti Raman hesitated, but when Ponni looked at the verge of tears, they gobbled the idili up. Then, saying something to Kutti Raman, Chimpu ran like fire towards the police station with a newspaper under his arm. At first, the guard at the entrance raised his gun like a stick when he saw Chimpu, but Chimpu held up the newspaper. On it was the Circle Inspector and Chimpu's photo. The guard was surprised, before he saluted and ran to tell the inspector. Chimpu was taken inside, and Chimpu found himself in a big room. "Oh! It's the super-chimp Chimpu! The one who saved Muni!". Chimpu began making some signs with his hands, in an urgent manner. The inspector was confused, and went to the ground to ask Ponni. He was told all that had happened- how Palani fell sick, how Chimpu was kicked out of the hospital, etc. Then, he took Chimpu to the hospital and took him to Palani in ward three. Palani's eyes filled up with tears, and the two embraced. Then, the inspector introduced Chimpu to the duty doctor. When the doctor looked scared of Chimpu, the Circle Inspector said "You see, this is not just an ape! He might not be able to speak English, but he has the intelligence of any man!". Then, the inspector asked on Palani's health. "He has liver and lung damage due alcohol and smoking. I'll try my best to fix him".

Then, the inspector went to leave. But before that he gave Chimpu a pass to let him visit Palani any time. As he left, Chimpu saluted him.

■■■

That day, no one expected an act on Chimpu circus. Everyone thought it was closed, but to their surprise, Kutti Raman began hoping around with his sign, and Chimpu began drumming. The biggest crowd Chimpu had ever seen flocked to see the circus. Then, Ponni and Muni came out! Ponni announced. "Dear friends, today Palani sir is ill, and is unable to come. Yet still, today we will start the show for you. There are no breaks for Chimpu circus! So, let's START THIS SHOW, now with brand new tricks!". Then, the show began. At first, Chimpu ran up, summersaulting all the way. He then said Namaste to the audience. Then, after showing a sign to Ponni, he threw Muni in the air! Muni imitated a bird as he flew up, then down, right into Chimpu's hands. Then, Chimpu turned into an elephant, and Muni, a mahout. Ponni acted as the announcer. At the end, all the earnings were given to Ponni and Muni's parents.

As soon as the circus ended, both Kutti Raman and Chimpu ran to the hospital with apples and grapes for Palani. This time, they were not scolded or thrown out by the people. The hospital people felt that the two were important! They only stared at them, as one would if you saw a monkey in a hospital. Palani became happy when he saw Kutti Raman. He was a bit better. Then, through sign language, Chimpu explained that the circus was still continuing! People gathered around, surprised that Chimpu could use sign language! Oh, how smart was Chimpu!

Chapter 5: Ponni's tale

Many days passed by. Chimpu and Ponni became good friends! Chimpu wanted to know Ponni's backstory. She hesitated at first, but then told Chimpu everything. It turns out, Ponni and her family came from a far-away place, where they mainly farmed corn and paddy. It was hard to grow crops there, but they managed. However, they lived under the iron fist of a landlord. They had to give a share of their crops and earnings to him, or face the dire consequences.

Then one day, a young leader came from the city. He called all the farmers, saying "You are all suffering, while you work for the evil landlord! You are all worse off than slaves! But, we can make a better life for you all! United, we can do anything!". The older farmers rejected the idea, but the younger ones like Kuppuswami (Ponni's father) joined him, and succeeded in overthrowing the landlord.

That year, the rain ceased to fall. The earth dried up and cracked, and the crops withered to dust. A monster of a drought had fallen over the land. Yet still, the landlord demanded his share of crops. What could the poor farmers do? They had none for themselves. So Kuppuswami and the others decided not to give him. The impatient landlord called all the farmers, and when he heard their decision, he was hopping with rage.

That night, the farmers awoke. Someone was throwing burning sticks at the mud huts. They burnt to ashes. The screams of the people resounded everywhere. It was no doubt who set the fire. The landlord. The Landlord's minions came and whipped, beated, slapped, and kicked the farmers.

Some died. Some ran with their lives. Kuppuswami and his wife took Ponni (who was a small girl at the time. Muni and the baby weren't born yet) and ran, far away. The cruel, wicked landlord frightened them, so they never returned. They became nomads, selling bangles, bracelets, etc. Ponni had been to many cities, and had met many people. She knew how to cook and take care of her siblings. Yet she never went to school, and couldn't even write her name.

Hearing Ponni's tale, Chimpu felt memories of his own childhood stir. The forest, his mother, the jungle animals… Chimpu felt miserable.

Chapter 6: Palani's childhood

Chimpu felt like it took an eternity for Palani to get better, but he finally did. He was discharged from the hospital, but not before he was made to promise never to drink or smoke again. Now, Chimpu circus had a whole new look! Ponni and Muni learnt to preform tricks, and Palani became nice, 100%! He no longer got angry, and was happy! Kutti Raman and Chimpu would be completely happy, if it wasn't for the times… the times where… where Palani sat, silent and dull. The sadness emanated from him. And then, disaster struck.

A big circus came rumbling into town. The posters showed it all. **"Gemini Three-ringed Circus! The one and best, forget the rest!"**. It had tigers, elephants, bears, lions, hippos, and what not! Clowns, globes of death, tightropes and more! This circus had it all.

When such a big thing came to town, who would even notice the little Chimpu circus? It was like an ant versus a whale! Palani was terrified, but did not show it. After all, if the sky was falling down, then could you hide? No, of course not! But even so, Palani was scared. His life had been one big tragedy, as hard as climbing a vertical wall, but when he finally finds a foothold, this Gemini thing comes and pushes him back to the start? Memories hit him hard and fast, like a speeding train.

When he was a kid, his parents died. They left him a plot of land. Then, his mother's sister came and took him in. Out of the good of her heart? Of course not. It was to get the land Palani's parents had left him. Palani was barely fed, with there being 7 other kids. All he got was scraps, if he even got anything! He wanted to go to school, but he was ignored.

Then, when he got smallpox, the witch of a stepmother sent him— Not to a doctor, but away, to an abandoned hut where no one lived. Exile, where he wasn't even given food or water. The man who dropped him there left him some pulpy medicine and a burning thing to put into his eyes. Palani wanted to cry, but he couldn't. He was too sick. Then, one day, when the pain became too much for him, he cried and cried, until he became unconscious. The man who left him there (Munniapan), said that the smallpox had become very severe, and that the mucus from his cough had to go, and on and on.

A few days later, Palani became conscious. He slowly recovered, but when he looked in a mirror, he was terrified. The smallpox scars were all over him. The entire village had lost lots of people to the disease, and the stepmother had lost three kids herself. She blamed it on Palani, who's life became unbearable. He was starved, beaten, kicked, scolded, and more. Sometimes he would wish that the gods had never spared him- that the smallpox had taken him away, so he wouldn't suffer any more.

One day, Palani escaped.

He began working in a landlord's house, where it was so horrible that he couldn't describe it. Palani got married, but his wife left him. Then, his life became meaningless. He began drinking, wandering around with no aim. Then, he met a little monkey, whom he named Kutti Raman! The two began begging for food. Children would follow the little monkey, and Kutti Raman would smile at them. Some kids threw stones at Kutti Raman, who would get angry. Palani would scare the kids away with a stick. Then, Kutti Raman would perform tricks, with Palani drumming on a drum he found in a rubbish heap. He would sing and tell Kutti Raman what to do. When Kutti Raman got hungry, they would ask for food, and head to the next house.

Chapter 7: The beginning of Chimpu Circus

It was many years later that when Palani met Chimpu. Chimpu was a resident in a veterinary ladies hostel. He was taken from the forest, and was loved by everyone. At first, the hostel warden wouldn't allow Chimpu. But after much convincing, Chimpu was allowed, and there he got his name.

Outside the hostel, there was a parrot named Chucky.

She could speak. Chimpu's cage was next to it. Chucky would call everyone she saw, saying "Hello, friend!". If the person looked, she would ask "How are you?". Then the students would say "Nothing, Chucky!" before bursting into laughter. After every class, the students spent time with the parrot. Everyone loved Chucky.

 At first, when Chimpu came, Chucky was quiet. So was Chimpu. After all, he was now locked up, and would spend the rest of his life in the cage! Slowly, Chucky began talking to Chimpu, but he still sulked. Eventually, he began smiling at Chucky. But he would growl and scratch any student who came near, so they all talked to him from a distance.

Two years passed. Chimpu and the students became good friends! But Chimpu was still sad, for he could now never walk around, swing from branches and laze in the trees. But still, he never showed it and learnt how to understand humans and their language. Then, the term ended. All the people in the college left, and took a photo with Chimpu and Chucky! They were sad to leave the two animals, but they still left. After that, the new students came.

Then, for vacation, all the students and staff left. One of the last staff members, Parvama, was fired. So for one week, Chimpu and Chucky starved alone. Chucky starved to death, and Chimpu couldn't handle it. He broke out, and began hooting like crazy. A few students came, and Chimpu attacked them. They screamed, and a person came and threw stones at Chimpu. He began bleeding. He ran to the roof. The police were called, and they came with guns.

That's when Palani came. He heard the screams, and saw Chimpu on the roof. He went to the warden, and bowed, saying "Please, give me a chance to take Chimpu". It took some convincing, but eventually he was allowed to go, along with a few guards. He went to Kutti Raman (who was chained in a cage) and took his chain. The ever-obedient Kutti Raman stayed in the cage.

Palani climbed up to the roof. He called Chimpu like how one would call a close friend. "Chimpu?". Chimpu growled. He smacked away the banana he was offered. Palani went and gently patted Chimpu on the back. He slowly relaxed, and Palani passed another banana to Chimpu. While Chimpu ate, Palani tied a chain to Chimpu. But he didn't attack. The two went down, and Palani patted Chimpu's wounds. The warden tried to pay him 20₹, but he refused. All he asked for was Chimpu, who was gladly given to him.

That's when Chimpu Circus first began. The three went to multiple grounds and preformed, and slowly the circus grew big, until it reached the modern day. That's when this evil Gemini Circus came, ready to topple all that had happened so far. Palani was scared. The future was uncertain, and the situation looked dark. The circus had come this far, with its three lively members. Now what could they do?

Chapter 8: Hopes and Dreams

The Gemini circus was inaugurated in an extravagant manner. The District collector himself was there to inaugurate it, and after that a procession of animals holding a paper cutout of India lumbered by. Hippos, elephants, bears- what did this circus not have? Now the kids forgot about Chimpu. The new circus was all that mattered.

As usual, Chimpu circus started at exactly 4:00, and ended before the Gemini circus. Palani boasted to the few people who came that in Gemini, there was no chimp like Chimpu! Plus, Ponni and Muni were now experts on most tricks. When the circus finished, Palani came and sat outside the tent for a while. By then, the first show of Gemini was over too. The ending music played in the background, grand and loud. Palani lay down, worn down from the show and his worries. Suddenly, a man with a smart suit and pant came with a few young people behind him. "Excuse me? Are you the owner of the Chimpu?". Palani got up with a start.

"Um… Yeah?"

"I'm the manager of Gemini circus. I would like to buy your Chimpu. I've been in need of a chimpanzee for a long time, and Chimpu is perfect! So, name your price.". Palani froze. Sweat trickled down his face. Chimpu was listening, and understood everything. He stared at Palani with terror in his eyes. Palani's fists clenched.

"Chimpu is my son. I cannot sell him".

"Name anything you want! We'll give it to you. Anything! JUST GIVE US CHIMPU!". Palani blatantly refused. The manager was disappointed. Why would this stuck-up fool not give him the dammed monkey? Palani saw it in the man's eyes as he left. He wanted that chimp, at any cost. Chimpu began crying. He was terrified! Palani went and hugged him. "I won't sell you to anyone. Don't worry" he comforted him.

That night, Chimpu didn't sleep. He was scared. Would the circus people take him and go? He heard the sound of the morning show far away, from the Gemini circus. Probably the trapeze people. He heard a lion roar. The Gemini world was so big, with bike riding bears, swinging parrots, elephants, tigers— and yet, Chimpu preferred his small world. It was his home, after all. He remembered his childhood in the forest… and then drifted away, asleep.

Someone came outside his tent. It was too dark to see who. The mysterious man dragged poor Chimpu into a cage. Chimpu tried to escape, to cry for help, but he couldn't. He felt a syringe get stabbed into his shoulder, and the world faded to darkness.

When Chimpu awoke, he was in a dark room. He knew he was in the Gemini circus. A big, round, pot-bellied man came, with a whip. The ringmaster! He tied up Chimpu and began to whip him, again, and again, and again. Chimpu cried out with pain. That was just the beginning.

Day after day, Chimpu was forced to do tricks, and was trained with brutal punishments. Glowing hot iron bars were dropped onto Chimpu, burning his fur. He was stabbed with sharp iron spears. He was tortured worse than any criminal. Finally, he came onto the show. He was forced to do many tricks. He became a mahout, riding an elephant. He wore different outfits. Everyone loved him! The children loved him! He got good food, and became fat. Chimpu ended up with merchandise, shirts, and more!

Chimpu hated this new world, with its colored bulbs, roars and squeals, screams and torture, kids on trapezes with shiny dresses, etc. He might have been Gemini's main star, but he wasn't happy.

Chimpu used to have one friend in this strange world: Little Meenu. He felt sad thinking about her. She was an orphan. Whenever people threw bananas and sweets at Chimpu, he took it all to Meenu. But then… One day, in the morning march of the show, Chimpu was riding an elephant, with a girl called Tara. Then came horses, leopards, lions, dogs, goats and parrots! Then, it was Meenu's turn. She climbed up on a tightrope, and began spinning, when she fell from the tightrope— and hit the floor. She never moved again. She was dead. The circus people just tossed the body into the trash, and announced that it was Chimpu's turn. He was supposed to ride a bike in a metal sphere.

 Chimpu hesitated, but the ringmaster came and whipped him again, and again, until Palani came and patted him. "ChimPu… CHimpU!". Suddenly, a pile of bananas appeared, with the sweet smell of a fresh idili— wait, what?

Chimpu woke up. He was in his tent, with Palani looking at him worriedly. The terrors of Gemini had all been a dream.

Chapter 9: The Gemini Circus leaves!

That morning, everyone got up late. No one had eaten dinner last night, and everyone was hungry. Chimpu became quiet, but Kutti Raman made a few gestures to show that he was hungry. Tears came in Palani's eyes.

He got up, with his best drum. Chimpu's eyes widened when he realized what Palani was about to do. He was going to sell his drum! Chimpu hugged Palani, but Palani got irritated and kicked Chimpu away. Everyone begged Palani not to sell the drum, but he went and sold it. He came back with some fruit. No one felt like saying anything. No one touched the fruits. Palani threatened to throw the food away, the food he had got from selling his favorite drum, and in the end, both Kutti Raman and Chimpu ate it all. "Don't worry" Palani said. "If we stay here, we all will starve. We cannot compete with the big Gemini circus. We must move somewhere else".

Then, it became four o'clock. Palani began drumming, but with his best drum gone, the usual "Thoom   thoom!   Thuba-thoom!"   became

"Thlooogns! Thpongs! Thaba-tham!" No one came. Everyone flocked to see the Gemini circus, who's starting chorus rang through the town. At last, Palani gave up and tossed the drum away. Then, the one street kid who had come also left for Gemini Circus.

With their last hope gone, the Chimpu circus had no other option. They had to leave. They had failed before the grand, great, gargantuan Gemini circus. No one slept that night, for the Gemini's booming music filled their heads.

The next day was moving day, they all knew. Ponni and Muni had to stay behind, for they could not come with the circus. Everyone cried. No one wanted to leave the two kids. But, what could they do? So that morning, Chimpu got up early, to give his home a farewell. But wait a minute… There was only half of the Gemini circus remaining! They were moving to another town! Chimpu could barely contain his joy. He dragged a (sleepy) Kutti Raman outside, and they both yelled for Palani! The plague was over! The Gemini Circus was gone! Now was Chimpu Circus's time to shine! The three hugged each other and danced. They could stay here!

When the final van moved away, Palani began drumming, his energy and joy overcoming the bad tunes of the drum, and turning them into a master's drumming! The banner was tied, and Chimpu Circus began again. At first, no one came. Then, kids, next grown-ups, and soon Chimpu Circus had gained its previous popularity! Palani snarkily announced "You will find no other circus like Chimpu circus! We are the best in town! So please, encourage our Chimpu and let us continue with the shows!". Chimpu and the rest performed new tricks, and soon, all was better than before the Gemini Circus came! Chimpu circus was back in business!

Part Two: Chimpu and Mittu

Chapter 1: The story of Thekkinkadu Maidan

"Whroom!" Cars zoomed past Thekkinkadu Maidan. Chimpu sat, watching the vehicles. Kutti Raman trotted next to him, with his chain around his neck. Chimpu had no chain, and he was free. But Palani knew that even though he was not chained, Chimpu would not run away to the forest. In his mind, he was still Palani's slave. Chimpu let his thoughts ramble, thinking about when he was a kid, in the jungle. Those were happy memories. But there were sad memories too.

Chimpu liked the city. Thekkinkadu Maidan was his home. It was circular, and was noticeably lacking trees, especially teaks. Recently, however, people had planted a few teaks for the next generation. Once, Chimpu had heard that the ground was a forest! That time, Sakthan Thampuran was king. He was fearsome, and everyone was scared of him. He ordered to cut the forest. An oracle said against this, saying that the forests are the goddess's braids. And, the king stopped cutting the forest— just kidding, he beheaded the oracle. Then, the forest was destroyed.

Chimpu watched, pushing past banyan tree leaves as sunlight streamed in. His mind was lingering on his childhood. Oh, he missed his parents!

Chapter 2: Mother and Father

Chimpu's memories came like a waterfall. Back in the forest, he had no need for memories. But now, he clung onto them like glue. Being with humans, he too became a thinking animal. He could now grasp human's two faces: The one he shows, and the one he hid.

Chimpu's father was the strongest animal in the forest. Chimpu was scared of him. He remembered his father, ever since he was a tiny baby! *'Do humans know about the family life of chimpanzees?'* Chimpu thought. *'They think they know everything, but they have no idea about most things!'*.

Before Chimpu was born, a chimpanzee named Jambu was king. He would kill any monkey who dared enter his kingdom. He was unchallenged, until a male Chimp came and began teasing him. He beat his chest, and roared. Jambu came, with one thing in his mind. He would kill this insolent Chimp. But, the new male punched him down.

A fight ensued, and it seemed to be a tie. But then Jambu was tossed to the floor. He fled for his life, and the male roared. Jambu was caught and killed, just like he had done to the many other innocent chimps. Chimpu's mother told him this story. It turns out that the new chimp was Chimpu's father! He was not as bad as Jambu, but no other male was nearby. Chimpu's mother was a good Chimp, and was close to his father.

Chimpu, as a child, was free. He would laze around in the emergent layer, swinging from the highest trees. The canopy was his sleep room. Cool breeze would make all the leaves rustle musically, like a lullaby of the forest. Sleeping at night wasn't an option. I mean, have you ever tried sleeping while all sorts of frogs, crickets, birds and bats singing their songs all at once? Good luck with that.

The understory and forest floor were where they got food and walked away. It was so dark there that even the sun's light couldn't penetrate that far past the leaves. The understory was where most apes sat, fishing for ants with a skewer. At the forest floor, the night would be aglow with fungi and fireflies. Like streetlights. But, it was the most dangerous time and place. Murderers like leopards and pythons scampered down there.

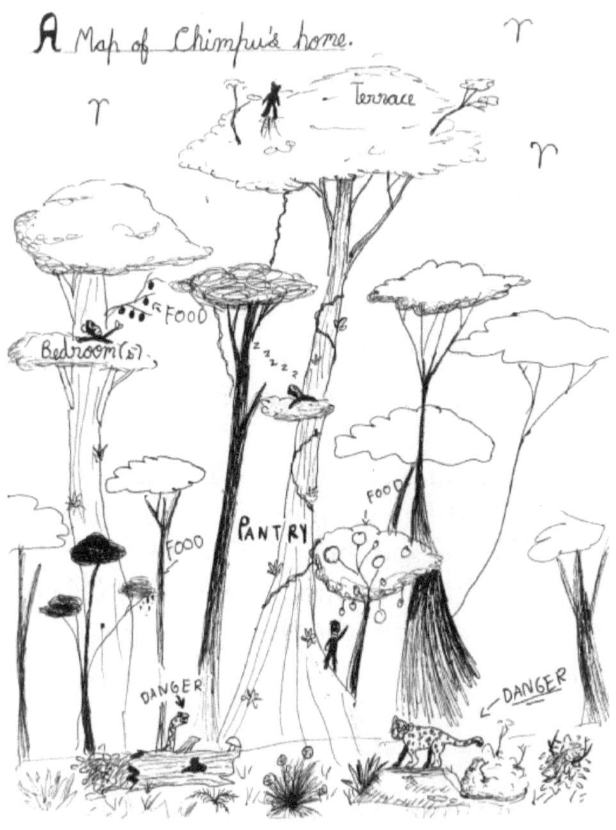

For a long time, Chimpu was adored on by his mother. She would play with him, let him ride on her back, and tell him stories. She could talk to him with a single look. The love of a mother and child is impossible to put into words, so Chimpu didn't try. It was a language of love, sadness, life, and joy.

Chimpu did not like his father. He was a cruel tyrant. You could see his darkness in his eyes. If anyone dared do anything he didn't like... well, they would be dead before you could blink. Father had more wives than anyone could count. In that case, humans were good, with their one or two wives. Chimpu knew that technically, Lord Krishna had more than sixteen thousand wives, but those were just myths.

Mother was a kind chimpanzee. She would cry as Father ignored her for his other wives. But she loved him. Chimpu looked just liked his father, and mother would beg Chimpu to be kinder than his father. She begged him not to be as evil and unfeeling as him. Chimpu would say "Of course not! I will spread the love you gave me to everyone!".

Chapter 3: Chimpu's childhood

Once, something happened that would scar Chimpu for life. A baby monkey played, running around and jumping happily. He accidentally fell into father's main territory. Father's soldiers grabbed him and dragged him in front of father. He ordered the baby to be… killed. The poor baby cried, and cried, but in face of father's cruel laws, those tears were no use. He was killed.

In this case, humans and monkeys were alike. They would kill their own people for no reason. They believed playing was a waste of time, and discouraged it. The kid was killed in a horrible way. The soldiers, laughing all the time, dropped the kid from the tallest tree. He fell to the ground, and cracked his head. Blood spattered everywhere.

When Chimpu slept, the image of the baby chimp's death haunted him. When he grew up, Chimpu vowed he would have no boundaries and he would never kill. Humans were just like Chimps. They fought first with stones, then with spears, then with guns, and then missiles. Through their wars, the environment was destroyed.

Humans were worse, though. Even though they had no kings, in their mind they were above all else. They would cheat and kill, if for their own good. They never thought of fathers, children, mothers or friends. They were just people to betray. Soon, monkeys would join humans. They were the ancestors of the humans, and were slowly becoming more and more similar. Not like humans cared. They disrespected their own kind, other animals, even the trees that gave them breath!

Because of this wars, so many animals and plants were extinct. The animals had to unite to save themselves from the humans. But, how could they? Tigers wanted tiger land, elephants wanted their own territory, so did chimps, leopards, rhinos, etc. When they fought like this, how would they unite? But unite they must.

 Chimpu shook himself out of his dreams. He was thinking too much. His childhood was much more! He continued thinking, thinking…

Chapter 4: Mother's love

Chimpu's memories of the jungle had a lot of playing. Chimpu and the baby monkeys were pretty rowdy, howling, jumping, and doing all sorts of shenanigans. They would steal each other's toys, steal and gobble up each other's candied bugs, ant-skewers and nut-sandwiches. They would squabble (until the grown-ups pulled them apart) and played with each other. Mothers watched over them, quick to help and scold if they fell or slipped. They would groom the lice-infested ruffians, who fell asleep in their laps.

Chimpu's mother would scold him, for he would climb up to the smallest, weakest branches, and bounce on them. Other monkeys would copy him. Some fell, others barely grasped the branch, and Chimpu's mother said "Chimpu, you are my only son. If you fall and die... then how can I live? Be careful".

"I am father's son, ma! I am a strong boy! I'll be a big king like father! But not to hurt and kill, but instead to spread kindness. Would you prefer me to be a coward, rather than a brave king?".

Mother hugged him and said " No mother would want her son to be a coward! You must be a good king, and I believe you will be! We are the cousins of humans, and we must not follow their path. We must eliminate evil, and be kind!".

■■■

One day, Chimpu and his friends where playing near the Mahogany tree, and they chased each other up and down it. They played, and soon the rest of the chimps were racing up the tree. Chimpu was in first place, going higher and higher. Soon, the hoots of the rest of baby chimps stopped. Chimpu looked around, confused. Where were the rest? He was too high, and had left the rest behind at the bottom. Chimpu shrugged, and continued up, until he reach the top. It was… beautiful. The tree stood above the rest, and he could see the peaceful forest .

In the distance, beautiful mountains touched the clouds. Below him, the green leaves shone. Birds twittered, and the rhythmic thuds of a woodpecker came from below. It was the most epic thing Chimpu had ever seen. He watched, entranced. Slowly, he came down. He was proud, as the first monkey to climb this high.

He ran, down. He saw his friends, who cheered! He saw the rest of the monkeys down, below the tree. He was excited to tell them his experience, and ran down the tree at top speed, when he slipped— he gripped the branches, but they broke— and he fell, and hit the ground.

Chapter 5: Mittu, The friend

Chimpu woke up, with his whole body hurting. His mother's tearful eyes stared at him. "Oh, thank god! You're ok!". Chimpu's friend, Mittu, was beside her. Chimpu felt guilty. His mother had told him to be careful, but his ignorance had punished him.

Father came, and scolded Chimpu's mother. He kicked her, saying that it was all her fault that Chimpu fell. Once he was gone, Chimpu asked for some water. He was too weak to move. Mother gave him some, and Mittu got some figs for him. He couldn't eat it, so Mother ripped the figs into small chunks and fed him. As per Mittu, mother had not slept nor ate until he awakened. Now, while he and mother slept, Mittu kept watch. Chimpu moaned, every breath hurting.

"Can't you sleep? Does it hurt?" asked Mittu.

"No, it's ok. You rest" Chimpu replied. But Mittu remained, like a true friend.

Eventually, Chimpu fell asleep.

Chapter 6: The World of insects

Suddenly, Chimpu found himself walking with Mittu, as they walked past an anthill. Chimpu hopped over a line of ants storming away from the nest. Workers and foragers stormed around in an organized line, marching on and on. A series of them carried ripped-apart beetles. They lead to a small hole in the ground, underneath which was a giant network of roads and chambers, filled with ants and larva. The queen was in there, hidden in the chambers. A few giant soldiers walked among the workers.

 A chimp was using a stick to fish out ants, and was munching on them. After all, for chimps ants were delicious snacks! Their little funny faces stared inquisitively at Chimpu.

Then, they were climbing up a tall tree, into a world of butterflies! Caterpillars chewed on leaves, as butterflies flew around gently. Each butterfly was like a separately painted painting. The caterpillars were green, and tried to look like a leaf. Chimpu laughed as one tried to mimic a flower. They were beautiful.

Chrysalises hung from branches, and eggs shone on leaves.

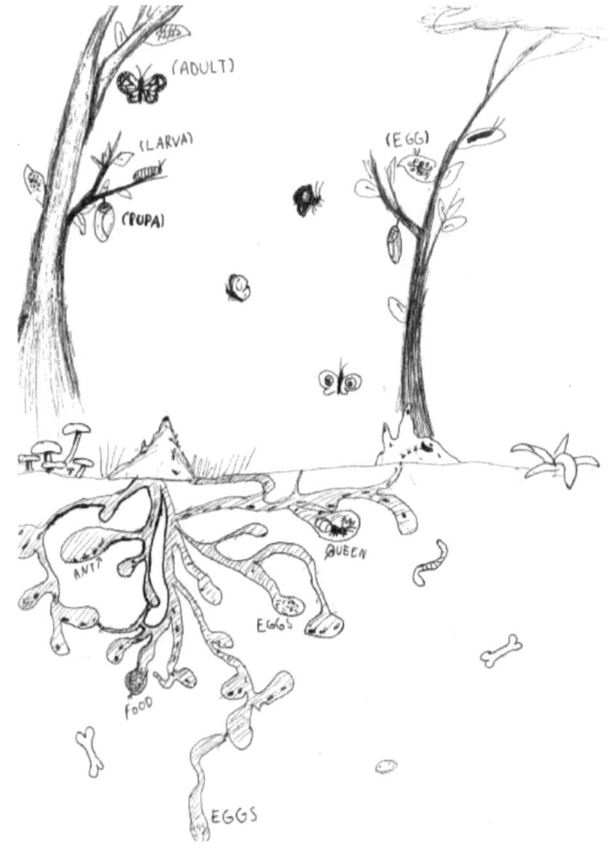

Soon, the two chimps watched from the top of the tree, at the view.

Suddenly, a voice said "Chimpu, what are you talking?".

Chimpu woke up, with his mother shaking him awake. It was a dream!

Chapter 7: A world without boundaries

When Chimpu woke up, his mother's face was watching him. Chimpu smiled at her, thinking how beautiful his mother's love was. Chimpu looked around for Mittu. Mother realized who he was looking for, and explained that he went to get herbal medicines. Apparently, everyone thought he was going to die, until a doctor came and said that Chimpu would live if he got some medicine. He had given some, and Chimpu got better. The herbal medicines saved his life!

It was father who got the doctor, but Chimpu doubted he loved anyone: Mother, him, anyone! Yes, Chimpu was proud that he was a son of such a strong father, and that he would inherit the kingdom. But... Chimpu wanted none, only love. If only father would hug him, talk to him, be kind…Like a real father.

Chimpu fell asleep, and was awakened by Mittu. He had taken leaves, sap, roots, moss, and a few vines to use as medicine (as per the doctor's orders). They tasted sour, bitter, and spicy. He ate them raw.

Through mouthfuls of weird ferns, he asked "Why did you go through this much effort?".

"It was no problem bro! In fact, it was fun! We found it in a beautiful place, with mountains and valleys! There were trees, ferns, and more! Elephants played in a river, and deer bounced on the plains. It was epic! As soon as you get better, I'll take you there". Chimpu smiled, thinking of his view on the top of the tree.

Mother appeared, and said "Chimpu, look what your adventures landed you in. I only have you, and I can't let anything happen to you".

After talking for a long time, Chimpu agreed never to go anywhere without his mom's permission.

Months passed by. Chimpu became healthy again, eating fruits and the medicine the doctor had provided. He became brave, and strong. He could run, jump, climb, cartwheel, dance, and swing.

One day, Chiki came. She was a cute, nice chimpanzee. She was… sort of kind, and could climb faster than anyone else. Chimpu's mother said that she would be a good match for Chimpu, and wanted her to be Chimpu's wife. Chimpu felt annoyed by this, and wanted to first spread kindness and love across the forest, and enjoy nature. Maybe later, he would marry someone. But not now.

Anyways, he pushed that thought out of his head and remembered that he and Mittu were supposed to be going into a jungle called 'Anamala'. He always dreamed of going into a deep forest, and this was his dream come true! He got his mother's blessings, but was then told to… get his father's blessing? The monkey who never loved him, even when nearly dead, had to give his blessing? He told this to mother, who said "You mustn't be as adamant as your father. Get his blessings". He had no choice, and went to his father.

Chapter 8: The forest expedition!

Animals, with their green homes, have a lot of good qualities. They had compassion, love, empathy. Humans had… um… well, some of them had those quality. Others… well, they had no humanity. They had no idea about animals and their life, and yet they said "We are the best! Animals are idiots!". Yet, they were ignorant to animal's hopes, their adventures, etc.

Chimpu (the modern one) shook out of his thoughts, a realization hitting him: He could never experience his forests and his memories again. He was stuck in a city, and while everyone there loved him, he was not happy.

Humans were filled with hypocrisy. They were… strange. For example, animals lived happily in caves, dens and trees. Humans needed over-extravagant palaces, houses and buildings. Animals were either fruit-eaters, meat eaters, or maybe fish or nut eaters. Humans… well, they ate what they want! But… while half of them die without food, other humans throw away food like toys! It was…

evil. Even vampire bats would feed other sick or weak vampire bats. But humans…

Chimpu didn't complete this thought, as he was sunk into his memories again…

■■■

Chimpu walked to his father's tree. It was the biggest in the forest. It was hard, for he had to be interrogated by a million guards. But, at last, he stood in front of father.

He was surrounded by lady-chimpanzees, and was playing with some babies. Chimpu was seething with rage. So father could love anyone, as long as they were the best. Chimpu's mother was one of the lower-ranked females, which was why father ignored her and Chimpu.

Chimpu's father looked annoyed at him. "Why did you come, you fool?". Through gritted teeth, Chimpu replied "I came to get your blessing. I'm going on a trip".

"Will you get yourself into more trouble, you idiot?"

Chimpu was quiet. "Fine, fine, I give you my blessings. Now get out!" said father, and sent him on his way. As he left in disgrace, the lady monkeys stuck their tongue out at Chimpu. Chimpu vowed to get revenge, storming out.

Mittu had arranged the travel, packing snacks and other things. Mother was waiting. Chimpu hoped she would not ask how the meeting went. He said that he got the blessing. Mother asked how father was doing. *"Oh, so he doesn't care about mother. But mother loves him? She worries whether he is well, yet he wouldn't even blink if she died. Really, he has no love."* Chimpu thought.

Then, pushing that thought away, Chimpu hugged his mother and set off with Mittu.

Mittu and Chimpu swung from tree to tree. The Anamala hill was filled with elephants, and was beautiful. They had paused for directions from some (scared) monkeys. They were following a map.

Being chimps, they swung from branch to branch. Eventually, they reached a place with no trees. In front of them, there was a large river. How could they cross? Chimpu drank some water, and notices a mango tree covered in vines. It had fresh, untouched mangos. Mittu and Chimpu ate up the mangos, and then swung to the other side of the river using the vines. There were lots of shrubs, and underneath was... a bunch of adorable rabbits! The little ones stared at the strangers, and , ears pointed, they hopped over to say hi. The grown up dragged them away, scared of the strange creatures.

Chimpu and Mittu introduced themselves saying "Hello! Don't worry, we won't kill you. We are nature lovers! We want to visit the... Anamala hill!".

The baby rabbits nuzzled up to them. The oldest head rabbit came and welcomed them. They were given carrots and tubers, and vegetable soup. They were welcomed. The old rabbit said " The river you cross is called 'Anamudi'!. There you can find many kinds of plants, endless insects, new kinds of monkeys (ones you have never seen) and lots of animals! The river begins at the top of the hill".

A mother rabbit warned " Be careful when you go there! There are-".

But the two Chimpanzees had already thanked the other rabbits and left.

∎∎∎

The two walked through the jungle. They were meant to be in a lush forest. But now, they were in a dark, deep wood. Chimpu was confused, and looked around for landmarks. Mittu noticed a lion tailed macaque, sitting on the top of a tree. The two chimps climbed up it faster than ever before, screaming for directions.

But the macaque was scared, and ran away. "Nooo! We're friends!" Yelled Chimpu, but the macaque ignored him. "STOP IT! WE WONT KILL YOU! WE JUST WANT DIRECTIONS!".

As they chase after each other, the screams scared away a bear drinking honey from a nearby tree. It ran away, with the bees screaming after it. "Honey thief!".

Chimpu felt like laughing. By now, the lion tail had returned, and asked "What's the problem?". They explained their plight, and the macaque nodded. He led the chimps to the tallest tree, where other macaques sat. The view was beautiful. You could see trees from miles away. The entire jungle was visible, and it felt like they could touch the sky!

"You see that forest, over there?" said the macaque. "That's where you want to go. It will take one week to reach there. Beware of the snakes, and also the tigers. There are even vultures that capture and eat baby monkeys!". Chimpu shivered at the thought.

"Thanks for your help!" said Mittu, and they both were about to leave when the head lion tail macaque said "You have a long road ahead of you, and both of you are tired. It is our duty to help you". Saying this, the two Chimpanzees were given multiple fruits, most of which Chimpu had never seen before. The taste was delicious! Then, Chimpu asked the macaques "Why are you scared of us?".

"Chimpanzees are usually pretty mean. They bully us, chase us, and beat us. Not you two, but others. They bully those who are weaker than them".

"We would never do that!" said Mittu. "We are on a mission to spread kindness through the forest!".

His words touched the macaques heart.

Chapter 9: The goddess of the forest

Eventually, Mittu and Chimpu left the macaques and headed south. They really began to see the beauty of nature there. The songs of cicadas and birds echoed around in a nice melody. The forest was so awesome. They happily walked through the forest, with no rain or snow, hail or gale, wind or heat, not anything to stop them. Rains did cause a delay, but they continued onwards. They met deer, who jumped and frolicked in the plains. They ate jamun fruits, and enjoyed a cool breeze.

They swung through the trees, meeting bats and owl. At night, the hoots and calls of animals kept them awake.

Then, one night, they saw something mysterious… a light as bright as the sun! IN THE NIGHT! What was this… thing? Both Chimpu and Mittu were scared. Chimpu had heard of forest gods and goddesses from his mother, and wondered whether this might be one. They edged closer, until they found a banyan tree, covered in twinkling light. Were these stars? This happened in an age before light bulbs, so it couldn't be them. Chimpu knew instinctively that he was in the presence of a forest goddess, in the form of a magic banyan tree. Mittu, however, thought it might be a dangerous monster, and that it was tricking them into thinking it was a goddess! They would come closer, and then the monster would transform and hold them by the hair, and drink their blood. When morning came, nothing would be left of them except their hair and nails (or so his mother told him).

"If it's a demon or god, there's no problem. Let's go and see! Anyways we'll never come back this way, so we might as well". Saying this, they went closer. Then, the tree began speaking. Chimpu expected something grand, but instead the tree said in a cheerful voice "Hello! I'm so lucky! Millions of fireflies live in my leaves, and animals from all over the forest come to see it!".

Both chimpanzees looked at each other, before asking directions again. They had forgotten the way to go, in all the excitement. The tree sent them in the right direction, and off they went.

Chapter 10: The hiss….

The travelers were reaching near Anamala now! And, for a chimp who always dreamed of going there, what better thing could happen? Chimpu and Mittu were joyfully walking towards the hill, when a stone hit Mittu on the head. Mittu touched where the stone had hit, and found blood seeping out. More stones launched at the duo, who ran and hid in the forest. They had entered a monkey named Jigu's territory. Jigu and the others came, with stones and sticks. They searched for Chimpu and Mittu, but they couldn't find them. They began laughing and calling the two cowards, saying that Jigu had won. Then, out of nowhere, Chimpu and Mittu leaped in front of them. Chimpu said "Sorry, we were on our way to Anamala hill, when we accidentally came into your territory. Please forgive us!". The commander said "LIES! LIES! Even if you came here by accident, the punishment is…. DEATH!".

"Sorry, we made a mistake. We will not repeat it. We all are chimpanzees, so why must we fight?" replied Chimpu.

The other monkeys did not like Chimpu's idea. "Surrender, then die!" they said. Monkeys came with sticks and vines to tie them up, but Chimpu attacked! Using their own sticks, the two beat them fair and square. There was a big fight. The other monkeys ran back to Jigu, but Chimpu and Mittu followed. Jigu realized that there was a problem. He apologized to Chimpu, who said "We accidentally entered your territory, and we realized our mistake and apologized. But you and your guards still tried to kill us. We have proven that we can kill you, but we will not. We forgive you. We monkeys should not be like humans, and should spread the language of peace and love, not war".

Jigu became happy. He and his kingdom was safe! He let Chimpu and Mittu stay for the night, and treated them well. The next day, before they set off on their journey again, he apologized for his bad behavior again. He promised not to be so cruel, and let the two continue on their journey.

■■■

Chimpu and Mittu were almost there!

Anamala was a playground for elephants, with lush green grass, rivers to drink and play in, and many new kinds of animals. It was epic, with its trees and nature. Bird nests were everywhere. Chimpu and Mittu climbed up and the moment they reached a comfy spot, they fell asleep.

"Sssssssssssssssssssssssssssssssssssssss". A noise came from above. Chimpu woke up with a start. What was that? He roused a sleepy Mittu, who said "It's just your imagination. Now let me sleep". Chimpu, despite how much he wished to rest, stayed awake. Then, "SsssSsssSsssss". There it was again! Chimpu looked around, and saw… A GIANT PYTHON! He shook Mittu awake, and the two leapt to another tree. The python followed. It tried to come closer, but it fell down, down, to the bottom. Mittu and Chimpu was scared. They felt a bit sorry for the poor python, but they didn't venture down.

Chapter 11: Baby elephant and friends

Chimpu and Mittu swung from tree to tree, and eventually slept. They woke up late, and quickly continued their journey, until they reached a paradise for animals: Anamala! There was a stream ahead of them, so they scampered down to drink some water.

Inside the stream, was a whole herd of elephants! As the others played and drank, the head kept watch incase danger came. Suddenly, the smallest baby elephant fell into the river, and was pulled away by the current! The mother elephant tried to pull him to the shore, but the current was too strong.

A Tusker came, but it was no avail. The poor baby was doomed, with a waterfall right next to him! The current pulled him closer to the waterfall, but then Chimpu came to the rescue!

He and Mittu dragged a large rotten log and tossed into the river, blocking the baby elephant from falling further down. Then, they twisted multiple vines together, making a strong rope. While Mittu tied it to a tree, Chimpu leapt onto the baby elephants back. He tied it, and then jumped to the opposite bank .Mittu began pulling. The old tree began groaning and creaking under the weight. The other elephants ran and began pulling the rope too. From the other side, Chimpu pushed the baby with another log, and the baby elephant was pushed and pulled back to the shore. He was safe! While the mother scolded and hugged the baby, the rest of the elephants thanked Chimpu and Mittu.

"No problem!" They said. "We are traveling to Anamala, and this is our first time here. Nice to meet you all!".

The Matriarch (chief elephant) said "Thank you, friends! We shall never forget how you helped us in this time of need. Someone showing kindness is new for us. In this forest, all the animals fight. Like this morning, for example. On the way here we met a tiny baby bison. It was terrified of us! But instead of comforting it, I took it with my trunk and tossed it away like a rag. I think it was hurt. Now, I got punished for that— Our own baby elephant nearly died! Thanks for showing us such kindness. In fact, as a present, you both can ride on the back of my brother, Dimbo! He'll show you around the forest". Chimpu and Mittu cheered. Never had they imagined that they would see Anamala on the back of an elephant! Yay!

Chapter 12: The message of <u>UNITY!</u>

That day, a meeting was announced between the elephants. Each herd sent a delegate, and they all met next to a lake. A Tusker made a loud hoot, announcing the beginning. Everyone was friendly, greeting and chatting to each other. Chimpu laughed and smiled. Laughed, because seeing all these formally dressed elephants in a meeting was funny; he smiled because his message of kindness had begun to spread.

Each elephant was different. Some had different numbers of toes, others had cool hairstyles. One had a strange bumpy tusk. Then, as night fell, the meeting was about to begin. Bananas were passed around, along with jamun juice. Chimpu and Mittu had some bananas on a plantain leaf.

Some baby elephants danced in the stage, and then, a lady elephant began the meeting. She announced that the meeting began. "Welcome everyone! Please take your seats".

The Matriarch said "Nowadays, this forest is divided. There is no unity between animals. Bears, elephants, bison, lions, leopards, and monkeys: All are against each other. Even within our own species, there is fighting. Because of this, we are weak and slowly hurting ourselves. We must stand united!".

The old elephants didn't like this newfangled talk of 'unity' but they kept quiet. "There must be a meeting with all animals! The Matriarch must take an initiative for that!" said one. And so, it was settled. With a loud, synchronized trumpet, the elephants announced the end of the meeting. After that all the elephant were served a delicious jungly diner. They had Cabbage biryani, watermelon juice, a main course of pumpkin curry, puffy pakodas, and honeyed apples. After that, they all left.

Chapter 13: Gorillas!

The next day, both Chimpu and Mittu went to explore with Dimbo. They walked through the jungle. Dimbo knew every inch of the place! In fact, every animal knew him! They would greet Dimbo with a "Hello" before waving at the two strangers on his back. Some were scared of Chimpu and Mittu, but Dimbo told them "They are the peacemakers who shall bring unity to the forest!".

The three of them saw grasshoppers, mongooses, birds, crocodiles, monkeys, snakes, etc.

Humans were not frequent visitors to the forest. "But", Chimpu said, "At any time they could attack, and turn this place into yet another polluted city. And if that happens, all the animals will die. I mean, where could we go? Could a tiger book a stay in a hotel?".

Even in the early morning, sunlight couldn't penetrate the forest. Sitting on an elephant while riding through the cool, dim jungle was an experience that would never leave Chimpu. They saw many rare animals and plants. It was a dream comes true for all of them.

As they walked, Dimbo said "Anamudi is the peak of Anamala. It's a very steep place. Going up is sort of easy, but coming down? Well, good luck with that".

Chimpu wondered how Dimbo would go there, if it was so steep. When they reached, it turned out to be steeper than Chimpu thought. He and Mittu clung to Dimbo's back. As they went, Dimbo said "Here there are gorillas! Lots of them! They are very dangerous creatures, and if a big one punches something even as big as an elephant, the punch would knock it out". Chimpu had never seen a gorilla, and wondered how they looked. Suddenly, he saw a movement in the trees. A huge, long haired body was there. It's human like face stared at them.

"That is a gorilla!" Dimbo said.

Both Chimpu and Mittu smiled at it, but it stuck its tongue out. It came down, each step it took causing a mini-earthquake. "Hello friend!" called Chimpu. "I'm Chimpu, and this is Mittu. We are Chimpanzees, from the northern forest!". The gorilla glared at them.

"May we climb to the top of the Anamala?" asked Dimbo.

"You may, but who are they?" It said in a deep, chilling voice.

"Didn't you hear? They are Chimpanzees, from the northern forest!". The gorilla turned at the two chimps.

Its tone changed, and it said in a friendlier manner "Ok then! I have heard Chimpanzees are as smart as hoomans (he meant humans, but Chimpu guessed he had an accent). Welcome, welcome!". It tossed them some delicious fruits, and melted back into the dark forest. The fruits were delicious, like honey dew. "Thanks!" he said, and, hidden in the greenery, the gorilla hooted and disappeared.

Later that day, the gorilla appeared again, to show the travellers a spacious branch to sleep in. Underneath it was a bunch of soft ferns, which let Dimbo sleep comfortably. Chimpu and Mittu could lie down in the branches, where a lot of leaves acted like a cushion. They slept happily.

Chapter 14: The honeycomb

The next day, the Gorilla appeared again telling the trio to visit the sloth of bears at the foothills of the Anamala. "Don't travel at night, or leopards will eat you!" he added.

So Dimbo and his passengers said bye to the gorilla, and then Chimpu asked "Wait… A 'sloth' of bears? What's a sloth of bears?".

"It's a collective noun" said the gorilla. Seeing their clueless looks, he elaborated "A collective noun refers to a group of something. A 'herd' of elephants is an example. Or a 'flock' of birds. In the same way, you have a 'sloth' of bears!". Then he disappeared back into the trees.

The travellers went and met the bears, who had been told by the gorilla ('could this gorilla teleport?' Chimpu wondered. How was he so fast?) about their visit. The bears served them a delicious buffet of honey, plants, fruits, leaves, a bit of strained mango juice, and some delicious curry. They had a gigantic termite mound nearby, which was a special treat for the bears. They gave some to both chimpanzees too. For Dimbo they served a banana curry, with a bit of leaf spices and fried coconut slices. Yummy! They also had a thing they called 'Jungle juice' which was a mix of mint, passion fruit, mango and jamun, with a little honey and cashew.

The little bears played, pawing at each other, summersaulting, climbing, and stealing Chimpu's termite pickle! One bear (chimpu recognized him as the one who had been scared away by bees while he and Mittu were chasing the lion tail macaque) laughed remembering how the bees had scared him. Mittu was currently being used as a moving bouncy castle by the smallest bear.

Finally, they had to leave. The bears handed them a bag filled with snacks, including, termite-mixed honey, some mangoes, a hollowed out gourd filled with leaf-sandwiches, and an entire hunk of jaggery. The trio then said bye to the bears, and continued onwards.

As they walked, Dimbo heard a buzzing sound above him. He looked up and saw a beehive.

He asked them for some honey (the one the bears gave him was mixed with termite). The bees rushed inside, and told the queen. She came out and said "Thank you for asking us first! Finally animals are allowing us to show hospitality!

In my world, the people worked hard. The women build and maintain the hive. They even protect the hive! The world has a lot to learn from us. The honey we make comes from our own blood, sweat and tears. And yet, without so much of a 'please' or 'thank you' animals steal from us. But you did not, and we are thankful for that. Here, take some honey as a present!".

Dimbo was given a few big chunks of honeycomb, and he and both Chimpu and Mittu munched on them happily.

Chapter 15: The Slender Loris

"We need to hurry!" said Dimbo as they trekked. "We need to reach Anamudi before nightfall". Dimbo felt like he was slipping down the steep hill, but he didn't give up. Not wanting to make it harder for him, Chimpu and Mittu came down from Dimbo's back. Dimbo took a large stick and used it to help him climb the slope. They reached a dense jungle, filled with birds. There were caterpillars on all the leaves, and smalls birds munched on them. Despite how much they wanted to talk to the birds, the travelers continued on.

Eventually, it was almost night. The horizon was smudged red by the setting sun. The birds were flying back to their nest. The animals were running back home. While they slept, owls and bats opened their eyes and flew on. Dimbo rested underneath a tree. On a branch above him, Mittu and Chimpu sat. All of them were watching with wonder as the bats and owls flew around.

Dimbo began stamping his foot, which was how elephants communicated over long distances. The shockwaves of his stamping would go on for miles and miles. Chimpu checked the tree for snakes. The trip was hard, but seeing all these beautiful animals, the kind bees and bears, meeting the elephants, seeing all the new plants and creatures (most of which Chimpu had never seen before)—It made it all worth it.

Eventually, as the nocturnal animals awoke, and the diurnal animals slept, the travelers, one by one, fell asleep. Only Chimpu remained. *"This trip was awesome! Getting down the hill will be hard, but at least we have Dimbo. How nice everyone was!"*. He missed his mother, who was the one who taught him to be kind. Look how far his kindness had brought him!

Suddenly, he heard movement above him. Leaves and branches were shaking. Not another snake! But when he looked, he saw nothing but the moon smiling at him. The light of the full moon was magnificent, making the entire place look like it was under a spotlight. The night-blooming flowers scented the air with a nice nectary aroma. Chimpu felt like the moon was peeking at him. The moon gave light with a cool breeze, while the sun gave heat and light. Suddenly, the leaves rustled again. Feeling scared now, he shook Mittu awake. "It's just your imagination! Let me sleep" grumbled Mittu.

So Chimpu woke Dimbo instead. He took it more seriously, and listened carefully with his big ears. When nothing happened, Dimbo trumpeted loudly, and a tiny thing fell onto his back. A slender

Loris! The tiny guy was shivering. There was an entire group of them, living in the tree. Dimbo realized that they were harmless, and apologized. Chimpu spoke to them, and became friends. The lorises slept the whole day, and when they awoke at night they were surprised to see their guests.

"You sleep peacefully," they said, "We'll keep a lookout. Plus, you have Dimbo to protect you". Saying this, the lorises retreated back to their home.

Chapter 16: The dance of a peacock

Early in the morning, Chimpu and Mittu climbed up the tree at the tip of Anamudi. They had finally reached their destination. They could see all the way to the other side of the world! The sun's light illuminated the forest like color in a painting. Chimpu realized how important the sun was! It helped trees grow (which gave them oxygen to breath), and gave everything color. Then, happy as a quokka (a smiling Australian animal that literally CAN NOT stop smiling!), they scrambled down. Dimbo already had his breakfast. They all felt like they had conquered the world! They were soo happy.

The loris family told about themselves, just before they went to bed. "We stay up all night, hiding in leaves so that no one can see us! We munch on insects, and guard the sleeping animals. Then, when the sun shone, we sleep".

Leaving the lorises to sleep, they began climbing down the mountain.

In between, they found a clearing filled with dancing peacocks. At first, the peacocks were scared. But when they realized it was just Dimbo and his friends, they were delighted and continued dancing. Chimpu and Mittu joined them. They all danced together, happy!

■■

After many days, the trio arrived at the bottom of the mountain. But this meant that the trip had come to an end, and Chimpu and Mittu had to leave. The three hugged each other, and the baby and mother elephant came with garlands to put around their necks. It was a trip never to forget, and the chimpanzees made lots of friends along the way. They all cried, and promised to visit each other again.

Chapter 17: Father's death

When he and Mittu finally came home, Chimpu didn't see one. He ran around, looking for his mother. Where was she? Then a soldier came and said

'Chimpu… your father is DeAd." .

At first, Chimpu felt no sadness. After all, father had shown him no love, disgraced him, and ignored him. But, he remembered his mother's words, "Do not hate, do not hurt!". He was led to his father's body, where mother and many other chimps were crying. The baby chimps were scared too. Death was not an easy thing, for a chimpanzee, let alone any animal.

Chimpu hugged and comforted mother, before preforming the ritual for letting father live happily in heaven. Unknowingly, he too cried. That deep was a relationship between a father and son.

After that, being the eldest son, Chimpu was to be king. Everyone began praising and respecting him. Chimpu hated this. People were drawn to power like moths to a flame. He did not want this, and so said that he would not be king. Everyone was shocked. Some called him a fool. Others said he had to. But Chimpu said "Being the king, I order my little brother to be made king!". He handed the crown to his little brother.

Chikki (remember her?) married his brother. She had no care for who she married, as long as it was a prince and she was a queen.

Then, Chimpu said "I am leaving here to explore and spread love and unity among the forest". He told this to his younger brother (who had more compassion than father) who hugged him and said "If you want to". Mother and Mittu said that they would come with him, and it was final. Mother wanted to see the world too, past the chimpanzees. And thus, they left.

Chapter 18: Mother's love

Mother, Mittu and Chimpu went to black-buck (A kind of deer) plain. It was a nice meadow, filled with frolicking herds of black buck. The three chimpanzees lived happily (and peacefully) there. Mother wanted to see giraffes, so they walked and walked, until they found a herd of giraffes. They were nice guys, with their long necks and spotted fur. They were scared of everything, but liked their new monkey visitors. Mother watched in fascination as they ripped off leaves from trees with their purple tongues. She liked these long necked fellas! The baby giraffes played with them, and Chimpu even got a safari on a giraffe's head! He could see all the way back to black buck territory.

It reminded him of Anamala and the mahogany tree.

But then, the travels and father's death made mother tired. Chimpu stopped travelling and tried to let her rest, but she became seriously sick. One day, she said, barely able to speak "At least now I can die in peace…". Her voice was wobbly. Mittu gave some medicine, but it was no avail. "Don't leave us ma! You are everything to us!". But, despite the medicine and pleads, she died that night in her sleep. She went peacefully.

Everyone, the black bucks, giraffes, even the birds came to weep with the two chimpanzees.

They buried her under a tree, and left flowers on it.

Finally, after days of crying and remorse, Mittu and Chimpu continued. Now, they were free. Alone. Independent. There was hope on the horizon. They had the power to build their futures! And so they set of, towards the horizon.

Chapter 19: The end of a dream

Once, when Chimpu and Mittu were visiting the Malabar giant squirrels, they came across a goa tree. Mittu was following a butterfly, so Chimpu went and began eating the fruits. He grabbed some extra for Mittu, and jumped down- into danger. He fell into a net, and hooted in terror. Mittu came running , and tried to free him—But the net became even tighter! Suddenly, a man with a tusk-like mustache came with a gun. Mittu tried to free him, but Chimpu said "GO GO! I might be caught, but you are free! Don't get yourself caught!".

Mittu wouldn't go, so Chimpu said "How will you save me if you get captured! GO!". Tears running from his face, Mittu ran back to the tree. The monkey catcher smiled. He had caught a chimpanzee! This would make a lot of money! He dragged the cage away, and Mittu screamed for Chimpu. But it was too late.

He was shipped to a town, where his cage was kept. The man tossed some food at him, but Chimpu refused to eat. He would bare his teeth at anyone who came nearby. Ever since then, he had suffered. Beatings, starvation, and suffering. He could no longer move freely. He was a slave. He moved, from master to master, until he reached Palani. He was transported in a truck, first to the hostel, with its parrot and starvation. Then he was with Palani, in the days before he settled in Thekkinkadu. Palani would punish him for whatever mistake he did, and spend any earnings on alcohol. Then, they settled in the ground. And here he was, without a chain, nor freedom.

Palani's drums dragged him back from his memories. The circus began. As he came, Chimpu wondered where all his friends were: Mittu, Dimbo, the macaques, the lorises, the bears, and everyone.

Would he ever be free? Did he dare hope? Chimpu prayed with all his might that one day, he would be free, and then stepped back into the circus—And into reality.

Part Three: Chimpu's world

Chapter 1: The beautiful, majestic forest

Mittu sat, on a mango tree. The branches were laden with mangoes, but Mittu paid no heed to them. Beneath him, birds pecked at worms in the ground. Deer nibbled on grass, before being chased away by leopards. A butterfly came to rest by his side. But Mittu ignored it all. His separation from Chimpu was all that was in his mind. Oh, Chimpu was his friend! His companion, his brother! How could he go like this? Mittu was still in hope that somehow he would get Chimpu back.

They did everything together- Explore, eat, swim, dance, play, etc. They shared all their memories, from the good, to the bad.

Mittu thought that even if Chimpu died, this much pain would not come. After all, he would die happily. But instead, he had been taken right in front of Mittu, and he was powerless to do anything to help him! Chimpu's calls of "Go, GO, save yourself" rang in his ears. It had been so long since then, but the memory was still there.

"I will get Chimpu back to the forest" He thought. *"I will free him, and relive the happy days together. I WILL SAVE HIM!"* he resolved.

That night, Mittu didn't sleep. He ran up and down a banyan tree, like a madman. His black fur was tangled and unkept. He climbed higher and higher. His blackbuck and animal friends told him to slow down, and warned that he might fall. Some tried to calm him down, but he shooed them away. Soon, he was at the top of the tree, on a tiny branch. It began to bend, but he paid no heed. He was about to fall, when a big brahminy kite flew and perched beside him.

"Who are you?" asked Mittu gruffly.

"I am a fish-eating kite, called the Brahminy Kite. Listen Mittu, anger and sorrow do not help anyone. Get rid of it, and you may find a way….".

Mittu recovered his senses, and sensibly took a step back from the bent, splintering branch he was standing on. "Sorry. The loss of Chimpu made me not myself".

Every bird, insect and animal knew about Mittu and his backstory. They knew Chimpu, the nature loving, peaceful, kind chimpanzee . The people who destroyed the forest hated him. And now, he was in the trap of the humans! Who knows what they were doing to him. When Mittu wondered that, tears came to his eyes.

"Mittu, for many years I have been soaring in the sky, watching the world. There is more ocean than land, and on whatever little land there is left, less and less of it is forest. Humans are destroying the few remaining green spaces on Earth. If it continues like this, one day people will be born in a world without forests, other than in paintings and dreams. We will resist this, and find your friend Chimpu. We will find him. I shall set up a search party. I will be with you on this journey too! Together we will find him!" said the kite.

Chapter 2: A parting

Every day, the city changed. No two days were the same. Roads were like a riverbed, with cars and vehicles flowing in and out. Every day, some or the other procession or strike marched across the road. The honking of cars was like the rumble of a waterfall. Sunday was the worst, like a river in a stormy season. Bulging like a lake about to flood, it was a rush hour. Street vendors were everywhere, swarming like ants.

Every Thrissur Pooram festival, a little circus would come to the city. Chimpu circus! During the festival, earnings would quadruple. But even they could not escape tax. During the festival, the circus barely had space to perform. And sometimes, big circuses (like that evil Gemini) would come.

At the moment, Chimpu wandered around, thinking about the forest. All his friends, the elephants, the lorises, how were they right now?

He longed to be in a forest with Mittu and Dimbo. He wished he could hear birdsongs and the gurgle of rivers, not the yells of shopkeepers and the honks of cars. He wished he could be free, but he couldn't. All that had faded from a probability, to just a wishful dream.

Now, his friends were Muni, Ponni, Palani and Kutti Raman. But Palani was growing old. Bigger circus managers came to buy Chimpu, but Palani would not let them. Chimpu became head of the circus, and Palani became a helper. The circus grew big. But Palani knew that he would eventually die.

One night, Palani was so tired. He hugged Chimpu and Kutti Raman, and then said "If I die, I don't need any money. Who will take care of you? So go join Gemini circus, ok?".

"No! You shall not die! You can't!". Chimpu was aghast. He had lost so much already, now he couldn't lose Palani too.

That night, he had a nightmare. He was climbing a tree with Mittu, when he looked down. He was so far up that elephants looked like ants. He turned, and Mittu was gone. Chimpu called for him, and the sun slowly set. Then Chimpu saw the unclear body of Mittu, calling to him, and he fell screaming all the way, "MITTUUUUUUUU!".

That day, Palani didn't wake him and Kutti Raman up. It was Ponni's wails instead. Palani was dead.

Chapter 3: Orphans

Without Palani, the Chimpu Circus was no more. It had died with Palani.

The District collector took care of Chimpu and Kutti Raman. The end of Chimpu circus became the headlines of news everywhere. People came to give presents and comfort to the two sad monkeys. For one week, this was the main headline. Eventually, people began talking of where Chimpu and Kutti Raman would go. Some said to another circus, others voted to send them back to the wild. Eventually, it was decided that the two were to be shipped to…. A ZOO!

Muni and Ponni could not bear leaving them. They cried and begged the two not to leave them too, but Chimpu was helpless. He thought of all the friends he had lost. Every time, he made friends, and left them. Oh, how sad he was! He was reminded of father's death. He couldn't even think of his mother's death. And what about Mittu? Had he forgotten his old friend Chimpu? Was Mittu a king? Did he have his own friends, and lived happily?

Chimpu remembered how helpless Mittu was to save him. He knew deep down that Mittu would come to save Chimpu.

Palani loved Chimpu and Kutti Raman. He loved animals more than humans. But when he was drunk, he would lose his sense . He would beat the two so badly that Chimpu wondered if he was going to kill him. But then, when morning came, they all became friends. He was like a father to the two. When the Gemini circus came again and again, offering higher sums of money, Palani didn't sell Chimpu. He had not a money based love, but a fatherly one instead. And now, he was…dead. Chimpu would be shipped off to a zoo , which was just another cage. Only there, he would have no friends, nor would anyone care about him. He was alone again.

Chapter 4: In the zoo

Chimpu was kept in a glass enclosure, with a lonely branch stuffed in a corner. He had no chain, but he couldn't even walk more than eight steps. Kutti Raman was faring worse. He was introduced into a cage filled with old monkeys. There was a baby one in there too. The monkeys almost ripped poor Kutti Raman to shreds. He ended up wounded and bleeding. The authorities dumped him into another cage, all by himself. No one treated his wounds, and he was weak.

Chimpu's fans stormed his enclosure, and it became the most popular cage. But all Chimpu did was sit in a corner and think of his free days. He hated it in here.

Meanwhile, in the far edge of Chimpu's cage, was an old blistered Chimpanzee. Chimpu asked him how he came here, and the ape said "I've been here since I was born. Taken from my mother. Here, people treat mother nature's creatures as just objects to wow at. As for you, you are the agent of the humans. You have no chain around your neck, nor a tiny cage, because you are a boss. The more exquisite painting in this gallery. I don't want to talk to you".

A mother monkey came and asked "Where did you come from?".

"I am a circus monkey. I originally came from the northern forest. My mother's name was Minkki, and my best friend was Mittu".

"Well then, welcome to hell!" said the mother monkey. "I've heard a school teacher say that humans build many zoos, and each one has rules. For example, there should be a forest like atmosphere and there should be cleanliness. The animals should be made happy". She gave a mirthless laugh. 'But here we are, unhappy, tortured, without cleanliness, and the best the authorities did to make a 'forest' atmosphere was to stuff a tiny branch into a corner".

Suddenly, the zoo superintendent passed by. Chimpu saluted him, and the superintendent was surprised. He gave a shake hand with Chimpu. Nearby news people took a photo, and it became the next day's front page photo.

Chapter 5: The investigation

Mittu's life goal was to find Chimpu now. The Brahminy kite (whose name was Kimo) did not simply sit. He flew from state to state, informing Mittu on the news. Mittu made a lot of friends, and they joined the search force. There was Dintu the deer, Peelu the fox (not a peel!), Dim-Di the rabbit, Kikku the crow, Jibloo the pigeon, Dingo the bear, Dimbo the elephant (remember him?) and Fuzzball the loris.

They all held a meeting to discuss how to prevent further destruction of the forests. Chimpu had united them to stop the cruelty of hunting, killing and selling of animals. To stop the destruction of forests. Mittu told them about how now, Chimpu too had been taken by the cruel humans.

They all took a pledge to stop the humans and save Chimpu. They were now all on the same team!

A lot of the older, other animals didn't like this newfangled thingy called 'Unity'.

One such monkey, Mimpo, was king at that time. He thought Mittu was a threat, and placed a bounty on his head. This made Mittu's mission harder, and he ended up in hiding.

Animals were supposed to be able to roam freely, but now, Mimpo was contradicting this.

Chapter 6: Training!

During a full moon night, deep in the forest, scuttling was heard underneath a gigantic rock. Mittu and his teammates were conducting a secret meeting, with Mittu as the president. Kimo was there as the aerial commander, along with his other kite buddies. A special team of birds was under his lead. Mynas, parrots, crows, pigeons, koels, all were present. 10 kites flew outside, spying for attackers and for Mimpo. Dimbo was there too. So was Jibloo, Dim-di, Dingo, Dintu and Fuzzball. There were two important things being discussed: Firstly, they needed a squad of birds to fly into the city and hunt for Chimpu, and also, a problem. Forest animals would reject any creature that came from the city back to the forest. They would attack and sent them back. Up until this meeting, no one had found a way for Chimpu to get passed this barrier. After all, he had been with the humans.

Kimo took his band of birds, and training began. A training camp in the forest? FOR BIRDS? Such a thing was never heard of before, but now it began. Each bird had their own skill. The pigeons had fantastic homing skills, which was why they were once used as a postal service. Migratory birds could fly over long distances, and remember the way back. All of these skills put together would make finding Chimpu easy as pie!

Chapter 7: Salvation

Before Chimpu was captured, he imagined a zoo to be a nice place, a bit like a forest, but with all the animals staying like one big family (and humans watching them). The leopards would get their own room, with a grassland, maybe a large tree to chill in, and a pool. Elephants got a lot of trees and fruits, and maybe a large grassland too. The deer would be antler-wrestling, and the rabbits would be chilling in their borrows. Bison would be in a deep, bamboo forest, and birds would perch on trees while singing. Each animal would have their own, perfect little place. Like a mini kingdom, all to yourself! He imagined a leopard in a spa, relaxing while food was served to him on a plate. It sounded like a good place. He and Mittu liked that idea. But when he actually came to one, he HATED IT.

He wished he could help the other animals, before freeing himself. But alas, that was impossible. He too was a prisoner, from his only crime of existing. It was insufferable. Stuck in a blank room, with no friends, no room to play, no Kutti Raman or

Palani, no… nothing. He would rather die than spend his life here, never seeing past the walls.

There was talk of transferring all the animals to a place called Puthur, but that was just rumors. The humans had said that from years!

Chapter 8: The bear

One day, bored out of his wits, Chimpu went to a nearby, barren, dull cage. It was labeled "BEAR". Chimpu remembered " Cheeman", the bear in his forest. He was addicted to honey.

 Once, he climbed a mango tree, plucked some mangoes and dipped them into a bee hive nearby. The honey covered mangoes were delicious! But the moment the bees came and began stinging him, Cheeman fell out of the tree, the mango plopping onto his snout. He ran all the way to Anamala to escape!

But the bear in the cage was as still as a corpse. It lay, quiet on the floor. People wanted to see it move around and do cool things, so they began throwing stones at it. The poor bear began bleeding. A guy poked it with a sharp stick, and it got up with a start. Chimpu went closer to its cage.

It sensed him, and the bear turned around. It was bleeding from the stones, its nose swollen and wounded. Its eyes were cloudy, and had sores all over its body. The bear collapsed again, and asked in a gruff voice "Go away monkey. What are you doing here?".

"I'm Chimpu. How did you get into this horrible place?" Chimpu asked.

"I was trapped. I accidentally came here, and now I'm a prisoner for life".

"What's your name?".

"Mungan".

"Where did you come from?"

"The Western Ghats!" said bear. "Even thinking of those times makes me happy".

"Could you tell your life story? I have nothing other to do than listen" said Chimpu.

"Sure. Not much else to do for me too!" replied Mungan.

He began:

"I once lived in Kuthiran mountain. It was called **'The Land of Bears'**. I was the prince, and boy did I love it back then. Everyone respected me, and I had not a single worry in the world! Me and the other baby bears enjoyed playing hide and seek, and jumping of the tallest trees! Oh, those were the good days. But then, once, when I was playing hide and seek, DISASTER STRUCK! I was hiding from the other bears, who had not found me yet. I was the best at hide and seek, and no one had found me then! I scrambled to a new hiding spot, when I fell—Into a pit. A group of men dragged me into a cage. I was just a baby then. I obviously tried to escape, but they shot me with a sleepy-dart thing—"

'Tranquilizers" Chimpu interrupted.

"Yes yes, tranquil-thingies," continued the bear. "I was shot three times, and I fell asleep. I awoke in Thiruvananthapuram Zoo. It was much nicer there. I actually had place to walk around, and the humans put in a lot of effort to make us feel comfortable. We were given good food, regular checkups to keep us healthy, and even were allowed to stroll in a wide open area once in a while!

 I met a female bear named Chinki, and we had many kids together. Soon, there were lots of bears everywhere! Suddenly we were put in a cage and shipped to here, leaving our kids by themselves. Then, Chinki died after a year. She died in agony, crying every day for her children. And now, I too shall suffer the same fate. Here, I have no space to move, food that tastes like dirt, wounds and diseases, and everyone throws stones at me". Tears swelled in Chimpu's eyes, and he wondered what kind of creature could be so cruel.

If only Chimpu could speak! No human could understand how animals talk. It was just noise to them. They could not imagine, nor did they bother to sooth poor Mungan's pain. This place was a jail for innocent people. They built jails for humans, but why animals? THIS WAS AN OUTRAGE!

Chimpu was seething with rage.

Chapter 9: Punishment!

Sundays were not holidays for the zoo. In fact, they were the opposite! It was Sundays that had the most rush. Mostly, it was children flocking to see animals from their separate schools. Teachers loomed over them, cane in hand. Some children were fascinated by the animals. Others were naughty.

One kid called Appu saw Chimpu and said "HEY! LOOK! A MONKEY!". "Will it bite?".

"Yes, it will. Stay away from the cage!" said the teacher. "Wait a minute… That's Chimpu, from CHIMPU CIRCUS!" said one boy. "Where's Kutti Raman?". A small boy came running to see, but slipped and fell. He was hurt, and began crying. "WHEEAAEEEEEEEAEEEE". "You won't listen to me when I tell you not to run, and then you cry when you fall?" said the teacher. With a crack of the cane, the boy stopped crying. Another batch of kids came in blue uniform, along with a headmaster. Chimpu wondered why animals had not made a human zoo, to see all sorts of humans! If that was a thing, then Chimpu would not be stuck in this hell.

He distracted himself with his memories. When he was free, there were boundaries they could not pass. With there being 6 other monkeys, Chimpu and his friends constantly crossed the territories. Once, complaint of this reached father. Chimpu and his friends were tied up, and he waited for punishment. But father let them go, only saying to try and do a reverse backflip. After a few failed attempts, he let them go. Chimpu was astounded by this sudden show of kindness.

Suddenly, the minister came. A MINISTER! Of… Chimpu didn't know what. Probably something important. Chimpu waved at him. Were these authorities blind to the suffering of animals?

Chapter 10: Suffering!!!

The zoo was slowly rotting away. People had thought on relocating the animals, but nothing happened. First, people thought to Peechi Dam, but that was 30 years ago. There was talk about sending them to a place called Puthur, but it probably would have the same fate. Slowly, the zoo rotted away, and the animal's situation only became worse. There was only one day where they could relax: Monday. When no human could come and pester them.

Each animal wanted its own home. For example, birds and monkeys liked trees. Not dried up chunks of trees! But alas, that was all they had. Plus, a zoo in the middle of a city is not exactly peaceful, the noise of vehicles disturbing all animals all day. Why would the humans never think of the animals when they make zoos?

The lions, leopards and bears had grown sick, weak and old. There was nothing in the King Cobra cage. There were no trees in the bird cages. And the deer… well, their condition was pathetic. Most of them were sick. The fox couldn't even stand, waiting for his death. The giraffes were nothing like the ones Chimpu had seen in the wild. Chimpu wished he could escape. If the animals united to fight the humans, the change would be worldwide. But here they were, stuck in a cage, waiting for death to come.

Chapter 11: Dreams…

Jingan, the lion, had a dream that night. Jingan had been there for a long time. He had a mate, Jingi, but she and his kids died. He was old, and weak. But in his dream, all the electricity went in the entire town! In the chaos, he managed to escape! He strolled out onto the road. All the cars stopped and stared. It was funny, how scared the humans were!

They locked themselves in their houses, peeking through windows. He continued towards his goal: the forest. The army and police came, but by that time, he was long gone. He searched, but all the forest was city now. He ran, and ran. He ate a cow on the way, which scared the people even more. Eventually, he reached the forest. Or what remained of it.

Most of the trees were gone, nothing more than stumps. Garbage was strewn everywhere. Jingan felt pangs of sadness, but at least he was home! He called for his friends, but they were all dead or killed. No one knew Jingan now, and he was alone. They roared at him, for if an animal spent time with humans, he would not be allowed back into the forest. He went back to the zoo, for he had nowhere else to go. The people watched as he trotted sadly to the gate of the zoo. It was open. But the moment he stepped inside, the gates slammed shut behind him. "BOOM!". He woke up, tears streaming from his eyes. Even lions could dream… and cry.

∎∎

Chimpu loved giraffes. They were shy, friendly creatures who never troubled anyone. They were scared of everything, with their long neck and legs. The giraffe here was in such a bad position that he couldn't even raise his neck! If he did, he would fall down. Apparently, the giraffe came from Mysore zoo!

 Chimpu climbed up a tall tree and talked to it. The giraffe said that he once lived in Mysore zoo, with his mother. But then, they were separated and the son ended up here, in hell. The time with his mother was the best, with its kind humans, big open areas and nice sky. Here…

The giraffe began crying. For such a big animal, barely any space was given to it. It couldn't walk, and move around. Chimpu tried to console him, saying that they would one day escape. But the giraffe knew those were just lost dreams.

Chapter 12: The guest

Thrissur zoo had a lot of rare and foreign birds. Eagles, macaws, ostriches, ibises, parrots, even giant parrots, the zoo had them all. They had drongos, pheasants, and more. Once, a new mysterious bird came. It stayed for a while, before saying "I am a migratory bird from Australia! We come here to lay eggs, and stay till the babies can fly by themselves. Then we fly back. Last time I came here, I saw you all. Now I decided to visit you, but I am aghast at seeing your condition. You don't even have room to fly! There is a fable, of some birds, who were caught in a hunters trap. They together flapped their wings, and escaped. You must be like that! Stay together, and be strong! Unity is key!".

Saying this, the guest flew away. The birds began talking to each other. Chimpu was watching this with awe. *"We can do it!"* He thought. *"WE HAVE THE POWER OF…. UNTIY!"*

Chapter 13: Slaves

As Chimpu wasted his days in the zoo, more and more of his memories stabbed him, and each time, he felt angrier, and angrier, until he was positively livid, towards the humans. Each animal in the zoo had a sad story behind them, of the trickery and cruelty of humans.

Take elephants, for example. Some have to load heavy logs onto boats. Every day. All year. Others were used as taxis, being whipped and injured to make them go faster. The weight of these slowly broke their back, until there was no spine left for them. And the worst was the temple elephants. People said they were so happy, as the elephants wore heavy jewelry for the sake of humans. It's like asking a boy to wear 800 pounds of ornaments, and then send him off to jog on the road. Temple elephants had to bear that without a word. And if any elephant tried to escape or get revenge, the blame was put on the elephants. I mean, all the humans did was kidnap it as a child, grown it as a slave, beat it till it bled, and force it to do heavy weightlifting for the enjoyment of onlookers. If one tries and hurts someone, clearly it's the elephants who are guilty.

Humans called themselves the smart animals, distinguishing themselves from all else. But if they were so smart, they would see the suffering of animals, and put an end to it.

Chimpu next visited the crocodile, Chingen. He was in a deep… pit? Calling it a lake would be a bit much for the deep, dirty pool. Chingen spent most of his time in the bottom the pool, so humans, cruel as ever, would hurl stones to make him resurface. Once, a stone hit him in the eye, and caused great pain. The crocodile stopped eating, as if on a hunger strike. No one cared, and no one even bothered calling a vet until he was on the verge of dying

The doctors did nothing but look and say "Yep, he's totally fine!". By the time they realized what happened, Chingen was blind in one eye. But, nothing changed, and people continued throwing stones at him. There was talk of importing more crocodiles to the pool, but nothing happened. So now Chingen lay, alone, and injured.

The injustice added fuel to Chimpu's hate of humans. He wanted to reveal the sad stories of all the animals here, but humans didn't even care about other humans (like the ones they kill in wars), so how would they care about animals? Even if they would help, how could Chimpu tell them?

Chapter 14: The Camel

The next day, Chimpu went to see the camel. He wanted to know everyone's story. Unfortunately, the camel was asleep, so Chimpu began walking back.

"Hey! Don't ya wanna speak to me?". Asked the camel. Chimpu turned back, surprised. "What? Oh, you're awake. Sorry, I just wanted to know how you came here. Start from your childhood, please".

"I am the ship of the desert" the camel begins, "And the desert is where I am from. Since I was small, I was told of the brutality of those evil rattle headed humans. They would use us for all sorts of work, from ferrying humans across the desert, to bearing loads, to racing. And once the tired camels collapsed from the work, the humans let him go and live the rest of his life happily—JUST KIDDING! They kill us and eat our flesh. Being a big, heavy animal, they use the excess flesh to sell, salting it and leaving it in the sun to dry. They are merciless rulers, forcing us to work and work, until we can't. We live to serve them, and die to serve them. They have no heart. In Arabia, where I come from, we have no stories of folktales and mythology. Just the pain and suffering inflicted by those evil demons, humans. It's inherited from generation to generation, like a bad luck charm".

Chapter 15: Hippo Beauties

Kimo's bird army failed miserably. They had searched the land, but found no Chimpu. Kimo himself had flown low, seeing the circus and temple animals. Whenever he talked to them (after making sure all the humans were gone) they all had the same tales of suffering and torture under the hands of humans. The whip of a ringmaster, the slice of a bullhook.

One example was Shingum and Shingi. They were circus lions, from Kamala three ring circus. They had been there since they were small. Training started early morning. It was brutal. They would be poked by spears, whipped by whips, and searing hot iron bars would be dropped onto them if they made a mistake. They were tortured day and night, for the enjoyment of people they didn't even know. If they had a chance, they would rip the circus people to shreds. But they never did.

One trick was for a little girl's head to be put in a lion's mouth. The lions could not bite. They did not want to kill the innocent girl, and if they did they would be killed too.

Kimo met African parrots, who had it even worse. They had to jump, swing, and fly through flames. One mistake, and they would burn like cinders. And if they did something wrong, the ringmaster would stab them again and again with needles. But, what could the parrots do? They were stuck there.

Kimo asked them all about Chimpu, but no one knew anything. Filled with pity for the animals, he turned to leave when the Hippo called him. The hippo too was tortured. He needed water, but all he got was a tiny puddle for him to sit in. Poked with iron nails, his show was to wear a bright blue jacket and skirt, and run around with his mouth open. A lady would offer him some food, and the hippo would open his mouth. The lady would then kick him and make him run again. Apparently, this horror show was the kids favorite. It was called 'Hippo beauty, human beauty'. But there was nothing beautiful about it. It showed the ugly side of humans. In fact, it was horrible!

Then, Kimo left. He flew above the city, in its hot smoky air. Below him, humans scurried from place to place. The city was ugly, nothing but grey. Nothing but houses, smoking factories, and featureless buildings. Where was Chimpu?

The birds organized a meeting at the stream. Kimo told about all the intel he had gathered, and about the circus. Then it was Kikku the crow's turn. She searched through cities and villages, yet had found no one who knew Chimpu. Once, when she became soo hungry, she went and stopped by a nalukettu house where a lot of people were preforming a ceremony. There was rice scattered everywhere, and she went and gobbled it up. The people said that it was a rare jungle crow, and let her eat. One guy said that the crow had the spirit of his father! Paying no heed to this, Kikku ate and flew away back on her quest.

Chapter 16: The death of the rabbits

Weeks passed by, and eventually Kikku found some information from another band of crows. Once, in Thekkinkadu ground, there had been a circus called Chimpu circus. She sent the information back to the headquarters, and was given orders to investigate what happened to the circus. Another crow named Kukken also heard about this. He lived in Thekkinkadu, and was close with Chimpu. He told Kikku everything, from how the circus began, to how it ended. He had no idea where Chimpu went after that, but promised to search. The next few days were tense. Would they find Chimpu?

■■

Chimpu was learning the backstory of all the zoo animals. The ones who fared worst were the rabbits. They didn't even have a cage, just a deep well like thing with a net on top. Once, a dog broke into the rabbit well. All the rabbits ran, and a guard came and shot the dog. Hearing the shots, all the animals became scared. The next day, all the rabbits were dead. Either from the dog, or the bullets. It was… so sad. All the animals couldn't bear it. Without caring the needs of all the animals, the zoo was killing them all. On the way to freedom, a lot would die in the middle. Chimpu realized this now. The sooner he freed the animals, the better.

Chapter 17: Zebra's sadness

The zebra was all by itself in its cage. It was pretty popular, and whenever the schoolchildren saw it, they began debating: Did the zebra have white stripes on a black body, or black stripes on a white body? Even the grown-ups wondered this. Chimpu went to meet this strange animal. When he reached its cage, the zebra didn't even look at him. It continued chewing the dry flaky grass. "PHOO!" It spat suddenly. It looked at Chimpu and did it again. "Phoo!". Chimpu was taken aback.

"Um… hello? I'm Chimpu the Chimpanzee. I came to meet you".

In a gruff voice the zebra said "Many monkeys come to pester me".

"I come from the northern forest. I was captured and kept in a circus".

"Makes sense. Monkeys are always clowns! They are so loyal to humans. I hate humans, so I hate monkeys!". The zebra glared at Chimpu.

"I love all animals, including man" Chimpu said. "But I hate humans who trap and mistreated animals. That's why I came to this zoo. To end man's evil and to rescue you all".

Less unkindly know, the zebra asked "And how will you do that? Can you even do that?".

"I CAN AND I WILL! I have heard the humans talk about Naranathu Branthan, the one who rolls stones up hills just to laugh and let them fall down again. I might sound like a lunatic, but we can do this!".

Sarcastically, the Zebra said "So all we have to do is set up a strike, a petition, and show the humans?".

"Listen, zebra" Chimpu says. "You are young, and have a lot more life left to live. If you say 'it's my fate' and let it dwindle away here, nothing will happen. But if you fight for it, you will achieve it! I know I and the rest of the animals don't want to spend the last of our days unhappily here, and I know we will find a way out. So do you want to join us?".

The Zebra looked dumbstruck. After a minute, he said "I… never realized that before. You have opened my eyes. I am with you! Now ask me anything".

Chimpu asked for his backstory, and the Zebra said "I came from Bannerghatta National Park, where I was born. I never saw a forest. The moment I was old enough to stop drinking milk, I was taken here".

Chimpu thanked him and left, knowing he had one more friend by his side.

Chapter 18: The Ostrich

There were only a few more animals to interview! Chimpu then went to the ostrich. Its enclosure was a bare, dry, muddy ground surrounded by wire netting. Chimpu had never seen an ostrich before, so when they ran towards him at top speed, he was overjoyed! He was not too happy, however, when they tried to peck at him through the cage.

"HEY! Chill out!" he said as he backed away.

"Why did you come here, you ugly old monkey?". The ostriches ran back to where they came from. After a few minutes, they came back.

"Hey, get rid of your arrogance. I came here to meet you. I have heard that you lay the biggest eggs in the world" said Chimpu.

"Yep! Plus, we are the fastest runners! Unfortunately, that's almost all we can do against humans. They torture us, for entertainment and for food. They eat our meat and eggs, hunt us for our feathers, and worse: hunt us for sport. They even use us as a tourist attraction! If it goes on like this, we will slowly get… endangered!".

"Wait, really? So your numbers are decreasing?".

'Yes' said the ostriches, "now GET LOST!".

"Easy there" said Chimpu. "Don't be so haughty!".

"Well then, don't rub salt in our already deep wound!" replied the ostriches. They took one lap around the cage, and came back. They seemed to be calmer now.

"Look at us. We are running animals. We are built to run. But we have no space to do so, no space to lay eggs, not even food! The other birds come and eat it all up before we can. We are suffering here" they said.

"Well, I am Chimpu. I used to be in the circus, but I'm now here to save you all. I will somehow help you all escape, or at least make your lives bearable. Are you with me?".

After a moments silence, the ostriches agreed. "Ok. After all, no plan is worse than a bad plan. At least then we know we tried. We are with you!".

Chapter 19: Snake friends

The snakes had their own little house in the zoo: THE REPTILE HOUSE. Ok, it was mostly just a big cage filled with smaller cages. Humans were always scared of snakes. So are monkeys. Chimpu still had shivers remembering when he encountered a python in the forest with Mittu. There was a python here too, but it looked miserable. There was an uneaten half dead rooster in front of it.

There was a chameleon, rock monitor lizard, anoles, and snakes. Each needed their own habitat, but all they got was a cage with a stone or branch thrown in. Not even with sand at the bottom!

Chimpu couldn't bring himself to love the snakes, but he knew that was a bad habit. So he asked the python "Hello bro! How are you? Are you ok?".

"Look at me! Do I look ok? When I was small, pythons ate deer, rats, bats, monkeys, and what not. Look at me now, with nothing but a simple EGG to eat for the next few days! My stomach is empty, and so is my soul. Oh, how I would love to eat a nice fresh monkey now! Squelch its bones, chew it's flesh".

Chimpu looked visibly alarmed. "Um… ok? So… where's your home?".

"Malampuzha forest. I had just eaten a large, yummy goat when a series of hunters came. I was unable to slither away, and so I was caught and tied up. I've been trying to escape this cage, but they made it strong". Then, tired out from all the talking, the python ate the rooster. "COCKODOODLE DOOOOO!" It screamed as it was swallowed.

Then Chimpu went to the viper. It was much friendlier than the python. It had a triangle head, with a brown body. Chimpu seemed to be a bit scared, so the viper said "I won't bite you. In fact, most vipers would prefer to hide rather than attack! They only bite if they have too, and even then they tend not to use their venom while biting a foe! That venom is for their prey, after all. But despite that, most humans kill us on sight with silly excuses like 'they are evil' or 'their venom goes directly to the blood!'. We would prefer to live peacefully, but if a human steps on us or tries to hurt us, and we bite back: the blame falls on us. Won't they ever think why we bite people? For fun? No, it's because they hurt us! We do it to defend ourselves, and get killed for it".

In a nearby cage, a few baby vipers began hissing. "Are those your children?" Chimpu asked.

"Yep. Gave birth to them myself". "Wait, what? I thought all snakes lay eggs!" Chimpu said. "Not all" the viper replied. "Only some snakes do that. Most vipers give live birth".

Then Chimpu visited the Krait . "Hello! How are you?" said Chimpu.

"Not too good. I have venom too! How are you?" the krait said. Suddenly, the nearby cobra hissed and called Chimpu over. "Heeeeello!".

"Where is your hood?" Chimpu asked. "We only raise our hood when scared" said the cobra. Chimpu read the sign above its cage.

> " There are nearly 3,000 kinds of snakes in the world. Out of them, around 300 are there in India. Out of that, only 60 species is venomous! Snakes are not the enemy of animals nor humans, but we say they are. Do not believe that. Snakes won't hurt people unless provoked or forced. So extinguish the myths, for snakes are the friends of everyone! They keep pests like rats out of our crops, they maintain ecosystems, and are very important! "

Chimpu read the signboard and agreed with it. '*So humans have some level of brain to acknowledge that! If only they acted based on that too!*' he thought.

Chapter 20: Good news!

As Kimo worried over how they would find Chimpu, a flash news came from Kikku the crow! She had written a letter, and it read : *'CHIMPU IS FOUND! He is in ~~Tr~~ Thrissur zoo! I learnt this from the local crows. I have gone to investigate'.*

Immediately, a meeting was made to discus this information. Mittu said "I had almost lost hope of finding Chimpu. I was caught up in my memories of the good old days. But now I have hope! WE WILL FIND CHIMPU!". Kimo said "We will find him, no matter what!". Investigator Dim-di the rabbit and Dingo the bear did some research, and found the location of Thrissur. Dimbo made a few plans, along with some emergency plans. Soon, a decision was made for Kimo to go himself and see thrissur zoo. They sent a message to Kikku, saying **"Stay in Thrissur. We are sending Kimo there, and he will need some help. Stay near the Sakthan Thampuran statue"**.

Kikku's reply was *"Sure thing sir! I will. But first I will go meet Chimpu!"*.

So she went and met Chimpu. He had an opportunity to escape, but refused to go. He wanted to help the other animals as well. He wanted to free them, or at least turn thrissur zoo to a green, free place.

Exasperated, Kikku said "Listen. I am part of a search party organized by none other than your Mittu! His friend, Kimo, will be here soon, near the statue of Sakthan Thampuran. I will be back".

"Listen, dear Kikku. The condition of all these animals is pathetic. They are dying here. I cannot come until they all are ok. Then, I will come with you".

■■■

Kimo flew over Kozhikode, then Malapuram and then Palakkad. He rested nearby the statue. He noticed how badly the garden around the statue was maintained. Covered in dirt and garbage, most of the plants were wilted and dead. The well nearby was ugly. *"Really"* Kimo thought *"Humans are the opposite of nature"*. Kikku came then, and told Kimo everything. He tried to convince Chimpu to come with them, but he remained firm. So the two went back to tell Mittu the news.

Chapter 21: Tranquilizers

When Kimo and Kikku came to take him to the forest, Chimpu yearned to go. To see his friends again. But Chimpu knew without him, the rest of the animals were hopeless. Their situation was becoming worse and worse. So he declined.

Meanwhile, the zoo superintendent was angry. This Chimpu was roaming everywhere, meeting all the animals. And if someone threw a stone at, say, the crocodile, Chimpu would roar and hiss at them. He was disrupting the zoo (and its income). So he planned to lock Chimpu up in a cage. At first, he sent two people. But when they came back scratched and bleeding, He knew he needed something else.

One day, as Chimpu roamed, he noticed a series of vets. Vets? Since when did the zoo care about their animal's wellbeing? Then, he noticed the tranquilizers on their belts. He realized something was about to happen. Something big. He climbed up the walls, trying to reach the main office. He scratched and pushed anyone who tried to stop him. He reached above the office, and saw the vets pointing the gun at him. He tried to hide.

More and more people came. Chimpu was reminded of how, in the veterinary hostel, he had broken out and climbed to the roof. It was the same situation now, only there was no Palani to save him. If only someone would call him with kindness, then he would come. Seeing all the guns and people, he felt a mix of terror, shame and sadness.

All the Chimpu circus fans came and pushed passed the police. It was chaos. The fans would not let them tranquilize Chimpu. News spread like wildfire. Eventually, the police said that Chimpu would not be tranquilized, and sent the vets back. The people tried to pacify him, but it was no use. Slowly, the people left until Chimpu was left all by himself. He fell asleep.

The next morning, Chimpu's photo was all over the news again. Both nature lovers and Chimpu fans came and began protesting, saying that the Superintendent who was intended on tranquilizing Chimpu should be fired. Suddenly in the crowd, Muni and Ponni came! They called for Chimpu, who got up with a start. He ran and hugged the two. Ponni gave him some food, and told him 'Please go into the cage'. Chimpu went and sat in the cage calmly. The crowd was relieved.

Chimpu's mind was a tornado of frenzied thoughts. Humans had even hurt him too. They

enslaved bears for begging, elephants for riding—
And monkeys for acting. When would this stop?
When would the animals finally be free?

That day's news was nothing but Chimpu. As if by
magic, Chimpu's near tranquilization had opened
the public's eyes to the suffering of animals. They
suddenly noticed the dead rabbits, blind crocodile,
cooped up ostriches. The nature lovers began
protesting that all the animals be relocated to
Puthur Zoological Park.

"Animals are alive! They are not born to rot away
in a city! They are born to live, and enjoy living.
They are important too!". Their strike revolved
around Chimpu. Chimpu wished to be in the strike
too. Whenever anyone passed his cage, he would
raise his arm as if he too was protesting.

The crowds yelled for the relocation to Puthur
Zoological park, and that it should be in Puthur
forest, not the city. As the yells grew louder,
eventually the authorities gave in. They announced
the new zoo, located in the forest. All the animals
heard this, and were ecstatic with joy. They were
going to what was (hopefully) a better place!

Chapter 22: The journey to the forest

The next day, disaster struck. Chimpu was missing! His cage was empty. Everyone panicked. Some said he was dead, others said that the angry superintendent killed him, others that he had went to the forest. Everyone began searching for him, even the animals, but it was no use. Chimpu was nowhere to be seen.

It had taken a long time for Chimpu to make up his mind. The idea of helping the other animals had been so deeply imprinted into his brain that he couldn't go with Kimo and Kikku. But now that he knew that all the other animals were going to a better place, where they could be happy, he was satisfied. His goal had (somewhat surprisingly) been achieved. But now that was finished, he had only one thing in his mind: Mittu. A friend so dear that he made an entire search party to find Chimpu! Chimpu would go back to the forest, and be re-united with his friends.

At midnight, he broke out. His black fur camouflaged him into the dark roads. He found a truck filled with spices on the way to Wayanad.

At first, the truck drove through plains. At night, it was so dark that he couldn't even see one step ahead of him. He thought about how dramatic his life had been : His days in the jungle, his mother's death, his capture, the hostel, His encounter with Palani, the circus, Palani's death, the zoo, and finally, here. He had got a message from Mittu, and he was going to see him again!

Suddenly, Chimpu found himself at the… beach? He had never seen the ocean before, and was completely shocked. The waves, the wind… Chimpu thought it sounded like a forest after the rain. Suddenly, a big… thing came and took him into the ocean, underneath which was… a forest? With animals? There were deer, rabbits, aquatic elephants, and more! Chimpu was shocked. And then the sun began rising, and the horizon turned red. Wait, the sun rising in the sea?

Wha- How, what? Suddenly, the entire ocean-forest jumped up, and bags of spices flew above him—oh. It was just a dream. The truck came to a sudden stop, and its driver came out for a tea break. Chimpu nibbled one of the spices. Mm, tasty!

Chapter 23: Up the hill, down the curve

The journey was uphill after that. There were lots of trees around the road, and mist wafted down from the mountains. It was heart-wrenchingly beautiful. Chimpu thought that wherever forests or any other of Mother Nature's landscapes were there, beauty followed. It was like a buffet of beauty! Not at all like human's grey blocks and cities. Chimpu watched as slowly, the truck climbed the hill. Eventually, it stopped at the top.

Chimpu looked down at the view. It was hypnotizing. The driver and cleaner boy in the truck were asleep, so Chimpu enjoyed the view. Suddenly, out of nowhere, the cleaner boy came up onto the pile of spices. He saw Chimpu. "MONKEY! MONKEY!" he screamed. The driver woke and took the jack lever (a mechanical device) and went to beat Chimpu. Grabbing as many packets of spice as he could, he ran and hid in a tree. The men searched for him, before giving up and driving away. There were so many miles left to get home!

Chimpu felt like he and his home were on opposite sides of the world. He wanted to get back home, but he was alone, and clueless on where he was. Chimpu wondered if the search party was still there, or whether it dispersed. He took a deep breath filled with determination, and set off to find his home.

He heard a Malabar giant squirrel, and tried to call it. But the squirrel ignored him. He saw burly looking rats scurry everywhere. The entire place was a sea of strangers, and there was not a familiar face in sight. Chimpu began walking, until he found a porcupine. He asked it if there were any monkeys nearby, but the porcupine didn't understand him and flared its quills. Taking the message, Chimpu ran away, thinking how strange this forest was! If no one could understand him, then how would he get back home?

He wondered about getting home. It was a return journey, and he was lucky to even be alive, but a solemn sense had overcome him. He knew that the forest animals would reject any city animal, and now that he had spent so long in the city, Chimpu knew he wouldn't exactly be greeted with hugs and joy. But Mittu would be on his side, and the younger monkeys would be on whichever side Mittu chose. So maybe even if the older monkeys rejected him, the younger ones wouldn't.

■■

Chimpu heard the call of an mottled wood owl. Humans were scared of it, saying things like the call of the owl means that you will die!'. Even Palani would mention things like that. But Chimpu knew in reality that all it was doing was calling for a mate.

Chimpu turned and saw it standing on a long branch, and smiled at it. Being in a forest made him calm, and he eventually fell asleep.

Chapter 24: Travel

Rays of light pushed past the trees, poking Chimpu awake. The song of birds was everywhere, and it seemed to give Chimpu power. Stuffing some of the spices he had taken from the truck into his mouth, he began swinging from tree to tree. No matter how many times he saw the forest, it never bored him.

It seemed like the wind, trees and birds were all singing together, a song that sang:

'The tip of the mountains,

Shrouded in cloud.

Trees and flowers

Sprouting all around!

The beauty growing

From the ground

In a visage of colors,

From red, blue, and brown,

The forest is our home,

So we say!

The beauty will–

Take you away!'.

Chimpu swung faster and faster, until he leaped and began walking on the ground. The crackle of dried leaves and squelch of the spongy water-absorbing ground came from underneath his feet. He walked, each step re-energizing him. He heard the thundering sound of an elephant, so turned and took a different path. He encountered a leopard, but escaped by climbing up a coconut tree. The leopard tried, but could not catch him. Then he continued onwards.

■■

A house crow went and told Kikku the news: CHIMPU WAS MISSING! She told this to Kimo, who told this to everyone else. Mittu was at first happy. '*He must have escaped!*'. But then he wondered 'Did those humans kill him? They are certainly evil enough to do so'. He was scared, and then remembered *The laws of a forest forbid city animals from coming back from the city. How would they get Chimpu back if he was alive?*'. But, whatever laws were bad for the forest must be broken, and Mittu resolved to get Chimpu back.

That day, yet another meeting was held, and this time, everyone came. Lions, rabbits, leopards, squirrels, elephants, bears, etc. The crows and birds came late. There were also numerous monkeys too. The moon came early into the sky, it's light patting everyone.

The elephant welcomed everyone, and the subject was announced: Could Chimpu return to the forest?

Some animals said "NO. We will not allow a stuck-up city monkey to come here!". They were the older audience. The younger animals said "NO! WE MUST ALLOW CHIMPU BACK! We must destroy the law. It's not Chimpu's fault that he was kidnapped! We must let him back!"

Chapter 25: Chimpu's return!

Chimpu swung from the dense foliage. He was nearing his home. The rainforest he was in was a familiar one! As he swung from the trees, he saw, in the distance- the familiar plains that surrounded his home. He was back! He was so close now! Oh, the trees, the plants, the birds, his friends; Everything was within his reach! It seemed like even the plants were happy to see him. He pushed past shrubs, and stumbled into the plain. He saw familiar sights, and began hooting and screaming with joy. He danced like a madman, calling Mittu's name all the while.

Meanwhile, high in the sky, Kimo searched for Chimpu. His sharp eyes could not find him. He was about to give up, when he saw a tiny dot dancing like a madman. IT WAS CHIMPU! Kimo was sure it was Chimpu, but then the tiny dot disappeared. Kimo ran and told this to everyone. All the animals stopped their work and looked for Chimpu. Mid chase, lions and deer stopped running and began searching together for Chimpu. Elephants tossed their food away and began trumpeting for Chimpu. Rabbits stopped their nibbling, and bounced out of their borrows.

Everyone was eager for Chimpu to be back. You could practically hear the wind and trees calling for him!

Chimpu was running. He found a familiar mango tree, laden with mangoes. He went and gobbled a few of them. Some baby monkeys were squabbling to get a mango. They were too small to climb up. Chimpu tossed the mangoes down, and continued. Eventually, he finally reached the forest, his home. News spread like wildfire. Some were ecstatic with joy, others were burning with rage. Kimo shot like an arrow towards the forest. And there was Chimpu! He hugged the monkey, and Chimpu said "Let me see those who want me to leave. I want to meet my friends. No matter what the cost, I want to stay here. It's my heaven, my home!".

Kimo spread this everywhere. Kikku the crow was bursting with happiness. "We must make the return of Chimpu a grand one!" she said. Dim-di the rabbit made a banquet of 101 dishes made of nothing but carrots, and Cheenkan the tortoise made a leaf-cake with termite and carrot stuffing. The frogs began croaking with all their might in a song, and the ducks began dancing (and splashing everyone). Nature had taken a new spirit, and the entire atmosphere was lively and happy.

But not everyone was happy. Some animals said that Chimpu must be thrown out.

They told of an elephant named 'Jinkoo'. He was majestic, with shining ivory tusks, flapping ears, and the strength of an earthquake. But he never listened to his parents, and was a prankster. Once, he fell into a pit and was taken to load logs. He was a slave, but a very good one. In his mind, he longed to go back to his forest. So one day, he took the mahout and tossed him into a river. He came back to his home, but the memories of the slavery overpowered him. He began destroying things, and was eventually was killed by the other elephants.

Chimpu's friends were scared. Would Chimpu be killed too?

The head of the foxes, leopards, lions and tigers said that Chimpu was not allowed back, even though their citizens said he was. King lion made it final. What could Chimpu do?

Chapter 26: A fight!

Chimpu's old strength had returned when he came back. His sheer willpower had got him back here, past the circus, past the zoo, and back home. But now, his home was split in half. One was with him, the other (including the kings) was against. The kings plotted to kill Chimpu. But Chimpu's supporters were ready to fight, even if it meant war. They began protesting, saying "Let the children of nature live in nature! Let this chain of laws go, and let our Chimpu come back!".

Both sides were ready, weapons poised. A war could start any moment. Chimpu felt sad seeing this. The thing that had kept him going all these years with humans was the hope he could feel mother nature's love once more. In the Thrissur zoo, he held onto that dream as he helped the animals. When they were sent to Puthur zoo, he was happy. There, he was a hero of both animals and people. And now, after hardship, and many bumps on the way, he was home. But his presence was not only unwanted, but creating a war! This was not what he wanted. "Don't fight" he said. "It's ok. I shall leave. I will go back to the zoo. At least there I have a place. Happiness and joy is not meant for an animal like me. I shall leave, and never come back".

Mittu was aghast. "Chimpu!" he called. "If you leave, we will come with you!".

Chimpu turned to the animals. "I wanted a forest filled with peace and love. I wanted to return to my birthplace. Is that a sin? I was tricked and captured by humans, and I fought my way back here. Is that a mistake? Should I have let myself rot away there?".

"You youngsters are the ones who always fall off the path. You came from the city; hence you are not wanted here. You are with the humans!" Roared king lion.

"Oh. Ok. When I was in the zoo, I met a lion just like you. A king , he once was. And yet there he was, lying in a tiny cage, barely able to move. I fought for those animals. For their freedom. So that at least they could have a better life. Is that a crime? I saw animals, working for humans. I myself was one. We were tortured and forced to work day and night, and if we stopped, we were whipped. Does that make those animals criminals? Who work intentionally for helping humans? Or are they innocent, forced to do things for their worst enemy?

I was tricked and left in a hostel, where I only had one friend: a parrot. When that parrot died, I broke out and went crazy. That's when I met Palani. I joined his circus so that I could get food, but also because he was a kind and loving master. So I slaved for him. Then, I met two innocent kids: Ponni and Muni. They were not at all different from our own animal children. I saved Muni from a bad human, and became famous. I also spread how strong and kind we animals are across the globe! Then, when I was in the zoo, I was shocked. I thought it was a nice place, where animals could live happily. But I found it to be a hell instead. I saw good and bad humans, and I also know that there are good and bad animals too. But is the fact I did all that a crime? Does it make me evil".

No one could answer that. Chimpu's friend began hooting excitedly, but Chimpu shushed them. "Control your emotions" he said.

Chimpu continued, saying "Look. We all are one big family here in this forest, enjoying all its comforts. Yet do we ever thing of our brothers and sisters, locked up in cages? They don't even get more that a morsel of food, nor do they even have place to move. They are literally rotting inside there. Yet do we spare a thought for them? They too were born in forests like us, and live like us. Is it their fault that they ended up there? Do they deserve a fate worse than death? I spent my time in the zoo fighting as a one man army to free the animals. Even in the end, humans approved of it. And, in the end I helped them move on to Puthur forest. Was that the wrong thing to do? Should I have left those animals there to die?

All the time I spent in the city, my mind and heart was here, in the forest. If you don't want me here, then don't send me back. Kill me here, so I may die happily. Mittu, friends, don't stop them or fight them. Let them do whatever they want with me".

Suddenly, all the animals except three joined Chimpu's side. The tiger, leopard and lion glared at Chimpu. Suddenly, Mittu spoke up. "And look at us now. Two sides, fighting each other. We are no better than humans, with no unity nor sympathy. Is this any better than with humans?".

Tiger and Leopard joined the rest of the Chimpu supporters. Only the lion was left. He turned, and ran away in disgrace.

Chapter 27: A new day

The sun rose in the sky. Trees gently swayed. The clouds swirled in the sky, with little water drops falling like flowers to the ground. It was a new day.

Chimpu and Mittu hugged each other. Elephants trumpeted as a kind of salute. Birds flew together in the sky. "One day", Mittu said "All animals will be free, no longer slaves of humans. There will be unity among all!".

"We have a lot to learn from humans" Chimpu said. "Humans have a lot to learn from us!" replied Mittu. Chimpu jumped and did a cartwheel, making everyone to laugh.

Chimpu looked into the horizon, at the beautiful forest below. His home. Chimpu smiled and said, "I am no longer a slave. I am **free!**".

PEACE
SAVE ANIMALS

About the Author

C.R. Das

C.R. Das is a teacher, author, scientist, social worker, and traveller who was born in Arattupuzha, Thrissur district, Kerala. He worked at C.N.N High School - Cherpu, National Institute of Virology -Pune, Kerala Agricultural University, and IRTC - Mundur, Palakkad, and served as Mannuthy Division Councillor of Thrissur Corporation for ten years.

He was a Member of the Calicut University Syndicate, a Member of the General Council, of Kerala Agriculture University, a Chairman of the Child welfare committee, a Director Board member of S.P.C.S, a Director Board member of Bala Sahithya Institute Kerala, and an Executive Director of Jawahar Bala Bhavan.

He is currently the State Council Member of PUKASA and Secretary of Pulari Children's World.

He has written 102 books for children in the categories of short stories novels, poems, drama, travelogues, and science fiction. Apart from that he had written 32 books for adults.

Contact: crdas13@yahoo.co.in

About the Translator

Austin Ajit

Austin Ajit is an eleven-year-old child from Bengaluru, India. Austin is a young naturalist, an author, an avid reader, a storyteller, and a child artist. Austin has published eight books, and this is his ninth book.

1. Grandma & Austin's Plant Kingdom
2. Austin's Dino World
3. The Day I Found an Egg (Stargazer series - 1)
4. Ammu's Earth (Translation)
5. Attack Of the Purple Blobs (Stargazer series -2)
6. Flying Dolls and Smiling Friends (Translation)
7. Come, Let's touch the Sun! (Translation)
8. The Ray of Hope (Short stories collection)

Contact: *austin06ajit@gmail.com*